THE SPIES WHO LOVED HER

Holiday Interludes

KATRINA JACKSON

Content Warnings

Physical violence
Shooting death

New Year, New We

____

one

____

"Ever Protocol, Beta."

Lane's voice wasn't quite a bark, but certainly not a question.

Kierra knew this one. She knew them all. She'd been studying for her upcoming exam like she hadn't studied since she'd almost failed Calculus sophomore year of college. When she passed, the Critical Materials certification would give her higher clearance and special protocols for handling sensitive data. Although she technically wouldn't be Lane and Monica's personal assistant anymore, her new responsibilities would extend some of the support work she already did for them and other agents assigned to them. Also, she'd be making more money. She'd had to remind herself of that paycheck each morning they'd been in Washington, D.C. and she trudged out to Virginia to attend the special training program. And she'd fantasized about all of the thigh-high boots she could buy with that money while she was bored out of her mind in her classes. She tried to imagine her savings account growing to stave off the cabin fever of wasting most of the holiday season in a nondescript warehouse where she and a handful

1

of other administrative staff listened to lectures that literally replicated the course reading materials.

But she'd finally completed her training. She knew all of this material. She was ready. So of course she knew that Ever Protocol, Beta was "Confidential paperwork. Needs B-grade clearance or higher to view. Must be saved with double encryption on secure Agency server," she said triumphantly.

Lane grunted, the only indication that her answer was correct. "SeaTac Procedure," he said, moving swiftly to the next not-quite question.

She frowned up at him. She realized he was only trying to help, and she wasn't a dog, so she didn't need a treat every time she got a right answer. But was a "good" or a smile too much to ask for?

"Give me an answer," he whispered, his eyes boring into hers.

She deepened her frown and scowled at him, "Water rescue with possible enemy combatants. Agent must take extra precaution to prevent civilian casualties." She ground out the words so he would know that just because he thought this grand inquisition was the best method to help her retain information didn't mean she agreed.

Or at least she wanted to grind the words through clenched teeth, but her mouth fell open and her breath spluttered out when Monica twisted her fingers inside of Kierra's pussy to rub that sensitive cluster of nerves that made her legs shake. She licked her clit with hard pressure and Kierra moaned, a small smile spread across her face as her toes curled under. She spread her legs wider – hamstrings burning – to give Monica all the room she needed to settle in and get very comfortable touching her exactly like this for as long as she wanted.

They were in their bedroom in the temporary Agency residence just inside the Beltway. The new place looked like a compressed version of their New Jersey house, which was comforting and disorienting all at the same time. Kierra had just barely moved in with Monica and Lane before they'd whisked her away to start the Critical Materials training program, not wanting to wait six months for the next cycle. The only upside to spending most of November and December in the most boring version of college was that Monica and Lane had traveled with her and after a long, boring day, she at least got to come home to the two people she loved, in a house that was almost familiar. Although Kierra had barely moved into their New Jersey mini mansion, so she hadn't had time to test out the idea of it being her new home. Every day that they'd been away, she'd tested the word out on her tongue in the facsimile house, acclimating herself to their new arrangement bit-by-bit. Part of that acclimating process was making new memories with Lane and Monica in the upper part of their house. Especially in her favorite room: their bedroom.

She was sitting on the bench at the foot of the bed. Monica was crouched between her legs, gently, albeit relentlessly, working her over with her mouth and fingers. And Lane paced in front of her, hurling question after question and clerical mission protocol after assistant security directive. She wasn't sure whose idea it was to quiz her while fucking her to make sure she could keep her concentration under pressure. But as her eyes fluttered closed, her head rolled back and the orgasm radiated through her in soft waves of heat from her core, she promised herself that she was going to suck the life out of them both in thanks.

"Last one, sweet girl."

Kierra moaned.

Lane had moved, his voice was low and full of lust as his breath tickled her cheek. He leaned over Monica to whisper to her. "What are your directives in case of an infiltration at our satellite site?"

"Satellite…?" Monica moved her mouth and began to suckle on her clit. "Holy shit," Kierra hissed.

"Command," Lane said, his voice exasperated. Urgent. He wanted to get this over with so they could fuck. She agreed.

Her voice was shaky. "Blue panic button locks the basement from the rest of the house. There's a keypad in a panel hidden in the east wall of the briefing room. Input code 87341 to alert The Agency and put out a distress signal to any agents within a fifty-mile radius." Her words trailed off in a breathy whisper and moans she couldn't stop. She was certain Lane didn't mind.

Monica's hand stilled and she lifted her head. "And then?"

"What?" Kierra gasped, bewildered and just on the edge of yet another release.

"And then what do you do?" Monica demanded in a tone of voice that made Kierra want to shrink from the intensity of her gaze and also splay herself out on their bed. She wanted that voice and her mouth to cover every inch of her skin.

"It's not in the directives," Kierra said, looking from Monica to Lane and back again. "They won't test me on that."

"Humor us," Lane added in a gentle voice.

Kierra licked her lips and sighed. She crawled onto the bed and took off her last scrap of clothing – a tank top that had become twisted around her upper body from Monica's distractions. She lifted onto her knees and watched as Lane helped Monica to stand. Kierra shivered when Monica leaned into his side and slipped her fingers, glistening with Kierra's juices, into his mouth. She could see the effort he made not to groan.

"After I shut down Command," Kierra said, her right hand moving to her sensitive sex, "and I input the distress code, I have to go to the panic room in the storage closet at the back of the basement. And I don't open the door until I see either of you on the security camera."

"See," Lane said, his hands already moving to undo his belt, "that wasn't so hard."

Kierra smiled. "But you are," she whispered, reaching for him.

When she took his dick, red and angry and already dripping from the tip, into her mouth, his face lit up. She kept her eyes on him as all of those grins and smiles he'd been holding back while testing her played across his face. She sucked him slow and deep. One of Monica's hands held him firm at the base and the other gently cradled the back of Kierra's head.

Yeah, she thought to herself as Lane's seed spilled onto her tongue, this test would be a breeze.

KIERRA STRETCHED her arms and legs out across the bed, yawning as she woke with a smile on her face. She sat up in bed and waited for her eyesight to clear. She frowned. Why was she alone? She threw the covers off her body and climbed out of the bed. She grabbed one of Monica's sweaters and pulled it over her head as she went looking for them. She padded down the stairs and huffed. They weren't in the living room – which wasn't a shock since it was mostly for show. They weren't in the kitchen, but she could see the remnants of their morning coffee. This house didn't have a Command in the basement, so she didn't open the pantry door. She retraced her steps through the living room and headed under the stairs to the hallway that led to the back of the house. The only thing in this portion of the house that mattered was the gym, her second favorite room of the house. Every now and then Kierra liked to pretend she was going to spend some time on the elliptical when really, she just wanted to watch Lane and Monica spar with a dull, aroused smile on her face.

She pushed the door open and there they were, barefoot on the practice mat, crouched low and circling one another with feral smiles on their faces.

"Good morning, sweet girl," Lane called to her as he reached playfully for Monica.

She swatted his hand away and moved just out of reach. He smiled.

"What's on the agenda today?" Kierra asked.

They both stopped, as if calling a silent truce, and stared at her.

"If we're not mistaken, that's your job," Monica said.

Kierra smiled sweetly as her face warmed and she rolled onto the balls of her feet, "Oh right." They went back to circling one another as she walked closer. "Well, I don't have my tablet, but if I remember correctly today is light, actually."

"How light?" Monica grunted just as she and Lane locked their arms onto each other's shoulders, trying to hook their hands behind the other's neck and gain some leverage.

"So light that I was thinking we could maybe start planning that *vacation* you promised me."

Monica grunted as she did every time Kierra mentioned this trip. Kierra couldn't tell if she was still angry, she'd negotiated for it in the middle of an operation or if she didn't want to go. Or, she thought – her abs tightening as a pit formed in her stomach – maybe she wanted to go on vacation but not with her. Maybe she was getting bored with her. Maybe they both would. Maybe she had been foolish not to have imagined this might happen. She clasped her hands behind her back, trying to hide her worry.

This new worry was an unintended consequence of moving in together. Kierra had thought that she would be floating on a perpetual cloud now that she had literally everything, she'd been dreaming of for three years. But she wasn't. Now that they were together, there were stakes – higher stakes

– because now, Kierra had realized, there was something to lose. Two someones to lose.

Lane and Monica pushed away from each other and began circling the mat again.

"Well," Lane said, standing upright and facing Kierra, although she noticed that his eyes were still tracking Monica in his peripheral vision. She'd straightened as well, but her body was still coiled, ready to strike. "We could do that or…?"

Kierra never got to hear his other suggestion as both of their phones began to vibrate, either a good sign or a bad sign, depending on her mood. Today she was tired, hungry and those worries were sitting in her empty stomach like lead. She frowned as they both stared down at their phones for agonizing moments. She was used to this; waiting as they received their orders. Waiting for them to give her orders of her own. Waiting wasn't a problem. But the silence as she waited was the perfect breeding ground for all of the fear that had just blossomed in her gut to sprout without her normal defenses to put those emotions in check.

"Change of plans," Monica said.

"I figured. What do you need?"

Lane looked up at her and smiled, "Have you ever been to Scotland?"

Kierra's eyebrows lifted and she shook her head.

"Well, great," Lane said. "Then we can get your vacation in-"

"No," Monica cut him off before Kierra could open her mouth. "She said it can't be on a mission. No work. Isn't that right, sweet girl?"

Kierra squirmed under the intensity of her stare. She didn't know what to make of it. Was she angry? Was she horny? Did they have time to shower together? She swallowed hard and nodded.

"Okay," Lane said amiably with a shrug. "Then we all need to pack for cold weather. We'll send a tech manifest within the hour. We need to be in the air in four hours. No less." He brushed his mouth across Kierra's cheek and squeezed her waist as he left the gym.

Kierra felt locked in place, her eyes on Monica and her stomach in knots.

"Is there something else you need?" Monica asked as she began to peel the gloves from her hands.

Kierra worried that if she opened her mouth, all of the questions and fears she felt would tumble out and she'd say the wrong thing or the right thing but in the wrong way. Her eyes searched Monica's face for any minute movement, some sign of what she thought or felt. But she saw nothing, and she felt herself deflate.

"Then go pack. And please bring a pair of practical shoes. I don't need you spraining your ankle on cobblestones wearing a pair of heels Lane bought."

Kierra nodded again, turned and walked briskly from the room. She didn't run even though she wanted to. And she didn't cry. Even though she really wanted to.

---

two

All of the field agents Mason Carlisle had ever known were so
different from one another that he'd stopped trying to catego-
rize them. They could be loud and brash, quiet and efficient,
annoying, charming, sarcastic, even shy. What distinguished
them from the average person was just theability to use those
unique personality traits to their advantage. But The Agency's
black ops division was much less diverse. They were the
strong, silent and lethal type, every one of them – except
Mason. Well, he was strong and lethal, but silence had always
been a struggle.

When he was recruited into The Agency, Mason had been a
typical bro – loud, brash, and kind of annoying. He had the
worst personality type for black ops, so much so that he'd been
shocked when They'd invited him to join the division. He liked
to smile, he made friends easily and he was just tall enough to
have a hard time blending in. But he'd said yes because black
ops was the most elite of the elite. So he'd adjusted over the
years. He smiled less, he spoke less and at a lower volume. And
since he couldn't shrink his large frame, he stood with an even
more rigid posture, intimidating most people around him so
they looked away. It wasn't exactly who he was, but it was

certainly who he had to be to do his job effectively. He had no problems making those changes professionally. The problem was that he had very little life outside of his work so Work Mason was becoming just Mason. And he didn't want that. To combat the full transformation, he made sure that he lived a rich interior life. He looked like an imposing, cold statue on the outside, but inside he sometimes felt like a volcano waiting to erupt.

"Hello, lovers."

Mason shifted in his seat at the familiar sound of the raspy voice in his earphones. He lowered the newspaper he wasn't reading to the table and looked around the small pub in front of him. He caught the bartender's eye and motioned for another drink. She smiled at him, he smiled back, and then shifted his gaze away. Outside, the sidewalks were churning with people, tourists and locals alike. Cars whizzed past. Across the street, the hotel where Monica and Lane would soon arrive was having one of its busiest days of the year as people arrived for the Hogmanay celebrations.

A waitress brought over another pint of beer. He thanked her with a polite but forgettable smile.

"This week we have an email from our faithful listener, and my favorite lover, Jarhead," the voice said. Mason took a sip of his drink and settled back in his seat, preparing to enjoy the way his words sounded in Tiya's voice; his favorite pastime.

He listened to the Bawdy Boudoir podcast faithfully twice a week, for work and pleasure. Tiya Randall was an unusual asset. Certainly there were better ways for him to communicate with his bosses, but he didn't care. He liked the feeling that grew in his breast when Tiya spoke, the way his dick stiffened as she read her erotic stories, the hope he sometimes felt when he queued up a new episode, and the familiar comfort hearing her voice gave him, no matter where he was in the world. So even when he didn't have a message to pass, he liked to send in a letter from time to time, simply to hear her say the words he'd written and feel some connection with another human being. This story was one of those; no clandestine meeting to schedule or intel to report, just an email littered with words he'd been daydreaming about hearing her say while stroking himself slowly to release in safe houses all over the world.

"Shit," Mason hissed.

Across the street, he watched Monica step from the back of a cab in front of the hotel. He paused the podcast and reached into his back pocket for his wallet. He grabbed more money than he owed, made eye contact with the waitress as he dropped it onto the table and breezed out of the pub. He didn't cross the street to the hotel. That would be stupid, and his career did not allow for stupidity. Not unless he was ready to be retired immediately.

Instead he walked two blocks east and took a roundabout path to the hotel's south entrance. He slipped into the service area, making sure to stay out of the way of the maids and porters who wouldn't notice him so long as he didn't disrupt their routines. He took the service elevator to the eighth floor and walked leisurely to the room the Agency hacker had assigned to Monica, Lane and their assistant.

The assistant answered the door. His right eyebrow lifted as he took in her outfit, a tight, dark gray turtleneck sweater that didn't hide her lack of bra, a tight pencil skirt, thick tights the same color of her sweater and very tall platform knee-high boots. It was not what he'd expected. Although considering the Agency gossip about her and the tiny scrap of clothing she'd been wearing when he saw her outside of the club in San Francisco, he really shouldn't have had any expectations at all.

"Carlisle," Lane said, coming into view behind her. "Come in."

He lifted the other eyebrow and the assistant stepped aside to let him in with a flirty smile.

"Thanks for coming on such short notice," he said, shaking hands with Lane.

"We didn't have a choice," Monica replied from across the room, her hands in her pockets as she stared him down.

"Have you swept the room?" Mason asked.

Monica and Lane nodded. They all sat in the room's small sitting area; Monica on the end of one couch and Mason and Lane on two soft chairs. Their assistant propped herself on the arm of Lane's chair, her chest resting on his shoulder.

Mason lifted his eyebrows, "Can we be alone?" He looked at the assistant.

"She stays," Monica said matter-of-factly, leaving no room for debate.

"She has enough clearance," Lane offered.

Mason shrugged. Clearance wasn't his main concern. That was something The Agency cared about. He was only interested in controlling the flow of information. As far as he was concerned, every op he ran was Need-to-Know and even then, he regularly withheld a certain amount of information to keep himself and his assets safe. For instance, he used Bawdy Boudoir for info drops enough that he knew there was an agent somewhere who listened to each episode to keep abreast of his movements just in case. But no one knew that Tiya was the reason he'd chosen the podcast. Because no one could ever know that he loved her. Not even her.

But black ops agents and field agents were two very different species in the world of espionage. This fact often caused friction in the field. So Mason didn't challenge Monica or Lane about keeping their assistant – who everyone knew was their lover – in the room. If they wanted to put her in danger, that would be on their heads. He got down to business.

"Have you read the dossiers I sent?" He asked. They

didn't dignify the question with an answer. He chuckled and smiled. "The Agency has been watching Elijah Moore for almost a year. I've been on him for two months. He runs a fringe European terrorist cell of Coming Dawn-"

"Sounds kinky," the assistant breathed.

Mason smiled and looked at her, "What's your name?"

She ran her tongue over her lips and leaned further into Lane's side, "Kierra."

"It's nice to meet you, Kierra," he said.

"Have you met me yet?"

Mason's smile deepened and his eyes shifted to Lane's.

"You were saying?" the other man said, as if their assistant flirting with him was the most normal thing in the world.

"Right. Coming Dawn," his eyes shifted back to Kierra's briefly, "is a global environmental terrorist group. But Elijah's sect is called Passage 14."

"What's their issue? Global warming? Oil drilling?" Monica asked.

"Meat," Mason said.

"Now you're just fucking with us," Kierra mumbled under her breath.

Mason smiled and turned to Monica, "They're a vegan animal rights organization. They're building their reputation by bombing meatpacking plants."

Lane's reedy laughter filled the room.

"It would be funnier if they hadn't killed half a dozen plant workers already," Mason said.

"Wait," Monica said, sitting forward, resting her elbows on her knees. "They're bombing the plants when there are people in them?"

"Yep."

"Don't they care about the *people*?" Kierra asked, incredulous.

"Not at all. In fact, based on Moore's speeches and online blog, the plant workers are basically demons."

"Jesus," Lane breathed.

"Why haven't we heard anything about this?" Monica asked.

Mason shook his head in disgust. "Because everyone they've killed so far has been an immigrant or refugee. No one cares." He saw Monica's jaw clench as she sat back. Mason watched as Kierra slid from the arm of Lane's chair and settled onto the couch next to Monica.

Monica's hands reached for her immediately, one hand resting on her knee, the other gripping her at the neck. Mason's throat went dry. He looked to Lane.

"What do you need us to do?"

"Elijah Moore and some of his closest allies are in town for New Year's Eve for a very rare vacation," Mason said.

"Okay. What are we trying to do? Get recruited? Seems too simple," Lane said.

Mason nodded. "Elijah Moore doesn't recruit directly anyway. That's been one of our problems getting close to him. He keeps his circle incredibly tight and he travels near constantly to visit his supporters and evade law enforcement. But I think this is a good time to approach them."

"Why?" Monica breathed, her hand tightening around Kierra's knee. Mason could have sworn he heard the other woman moan at the pressure.

He swallowed and continued. "We think their defenses are down. They've had a few successful attacks recently and agents sitting on cells all over Europe have reported that they seem to be recruiting more. All of them. Something big is coming. And we think Elijah might feel secure and insulated enough for us to slip through his defenses."

"How?" Lane asked impatiently. "Or is that why you invited us here? Black ops need us regular field agents to concoct a plan for you?"

Lane's voice was teasing. Other black ops operatives might have been offended by his insinuation, but Mason was different. He looked Lane squarely in the eyes and smiled, "I have a plan, but I need your help executing it."

Lane raised an eyebrow and smirked, "We're all ears."

"Elijah Moore doesn't recruit directly, so it would take months, maybe years to get to him. But there is another way to get into his orbit. Surveillance says that while Elijah is very cautious about letting his followers get too close to him, he's much less discerning about his sexual partners."

Kierra laughed, a bright tinkle of a sound. "Figures," she whispered.

"I need your help getting his attention and getting him alone so my team can do what we do best."

"Why do you need us if you already have a team on site?" Monica asked. Her voice was strained. Her hungry eyes on Kierra's profile.

Mason huffed out a laugh, "Two reasons. First, Elijah might have fewer bodyguards but he's not completely alone. His wife or his deputy are with him near constantly and suspicious as hell. And second," he paused to look Kierra in the eye, "This is your specialty. My team is great at surveillance and covert transpo. We're under the radar. But you two," he looked at Monica and then Lane, "are the best at getting attention and using it to complete the mission. I've read all of your mission reports."

Lane smiled, "You sound like a fan."

Mason shrugged, "I respect good work. You two do good work. And most importantly, you work fast. I know our strengths in ops. We could embed for months and maybe get to him. That was the original plan when They brought me on. But things have changed."

Lane motioned for him to continue.

"Two weeks ago we intercepted a phone call with Elijah and an associate in Germany. Passage 14 is planning another attack early in the New Year. We need to take him into custody now. We need the details."

"So what do you want us to do? Proposition him at the grocery store?" Monica asked.

Mason laughed, "You know, if he did his own grocery shopping, I think you two could have made that work. But on that same phone call, Elijah said that he would be unavailable for a bit around his annual New Year's Eve party."

"So we're looking to get an invite? Got it," Lane said.

"But we have a time constraint. We need to get him now. We have to operate under the assumption that he won't be this available again until next New Year's Eve. And we just can't wait that long."

Lane nodded, "Then all we need is to know what turns him on and we'll handle the rest."

Mason smiled, "He and his wife like couples."

Lane chuckled and sat back in his chair, "Say no more. This really is our specialty."

"I agree. And I was going to send you in alone, but I have another idea," Mason said, turning to Kierra. "How would you like to play my wife for a while?"

She smiled at the word 'play'.

"No," Monica said.

"Two couples are better than one," Mason breathed, not taking his eyes off of Kierra.

"I agree," Monica said.

Mason lifted his eyes to her.

"You can have Lane. Kierra stays with me," she said.

When he turned to Lane the man had a dirty smile on his face. "Unless you have any objections."

Mason laughed. "No, sir," he replied.

"Mmmm," Kierra hummed. "Say it again."

---

three

Kierra strutted out of the bedroom in another pair of knee-high boots and her favorite green jersey dress that almost covered her thighs. She swiveled her head to look at herself in every shiny surface.

Monica turned to her and began shaking her head before she even had a good look at the outfit. "Absolutely not," she said.

Kierra stopped mid-step and threw her hands out to either side. "I've worn this to work before," she said.

Lane was slipping a pair of cufflinks on. He chuckled softly to himself, no doubt remembering the last time she'd worn this particular dress. She'd barely made it into Command before they'd pounced on her and she'd let them with excited giggles. They'd lost the better part of the afternoon breaking their prohibition against too much sex in the office. Monica loved this dress. It was part of the reason Kierra had packed it and she'd expected it to go over well. Monica's glare and emphatic head shake hadn't even crossed her mind as a possibility.

"We're supposed to be a regular couple of tourists

wandering around Europe. Nothing about that dress is regular."

Kierra put her hands on her hips, "This dress takes up no room in my suitcase and the boots barely have a heel!"

Lane burst into laughter. Monica rolled her eyes. "Are you wearing underwear, Kierra?" Kierra frowned and her eyes shifted away guiltily. "You don't need to answer. I can see. It's barely thirty degrees outside. You need to go change," Monica said definitively.

Kierra turned to Lane, who looked dapper in a perfectly cut gray suit and overcoat that made his ice-blue eyes look piercing and near-terrifying.

"Why does he get to look like himself?" She mumbled petulantly.

Lane stood from his chair. He circled her and moved the hair from her neck to lick at her pulse. She gasped softly. "Because I'm the husband of a very rich financier who keeps me in all of the best designers," Lane said, whispering his cover into her ear.

"Why would people like that want to hang out with the leader of a fringe environmental terrorist cell?" She asked. Her breath hitched as he splayed his hand over her stomach, pulling her back into his body.

"Because," he said and nipped at her earlobe, "Rich people are always looking for flashy ways to waste their money. Terrorism is just an expensive hobby."

His other hand moved to turn her face so that she was facing him. He kissed her hard, stroking his tongue against hers in a familiar desperation. She moaned into his mouth and tried to turn around, wanting to climb his tall, lanky body and rip the expensive suit off of him, one piece of clothing at a time. But that hand on her abdomen held her fast, pulling her back into the gentle mound of his growing erection. It was a lovely goodbye.

Just as quickly as he'd kissed her, the pressure of his mouth disappeared. She leaned forward, trying to recapture his lips, but he backed away. She swayed slightly when he let her go. He licked his lips and turned to Monica with a devilish grin and a wink. "You two be good," he said as he walked from their room.

Kierra watched the door for seconds after Lane had gone, taking the time to slow her breathing. When she finally tore her eyes away, she found Monica staring at her with those same impassive eyes. After the heat of Lane's body and kiss, that glare felt like being dunked into a pool of ice water. She sighed sadly. "I'll go change."

In the bedroom she stood in front of the closet, moving the hangers back and forth, not really seeing any of the clothes in front of her. That feeling in her stomach had returned and the effort it took to stop the tears building at the back of her eyes from falling was sapping all of her energy. She wanted to crawl into the bed behind her and sleep until the world made sense again. She didn't hear Monica come into the room. She didn't even realize she was there until Monica's body heat caught her attention.

Monica moved Kierra's hair from her shoulder and leaned forward, licking her pulse at the exact place where Lane's tongue had swiped across her skin. "What's wrong?"

Kierra shook her head immediately, "Nothing. Jet lag."

"Is it nothing or is it jet lag?" Monica's breath rustled the hair at the nape of Kierra's neck. Her lips whispered across her skin. Kierra shivered. "Or is it something else?"

This was her chance, she thought. She should ask Monica all of the questions that had been littering her brain while she was bored in D.C., growing bigger and more terrifying each idle minute. But she didn't. "We don't have to go on vacation," she whispered quietly. "We travel a lot already. We can just stay at home. Staycation or whatever."

"Why would we do that?" Monica whispered, her hands traveling down Kierra's sides.

She chewed her lip and tried to find a way to phrase her response to change the answer she felt certain Monica would give. But she couldn't. She closed her eyes and whispered the words. "Because you don't want to," she said. But what she meant was, "because you don't want me."

Kierra was always worried that she was more invested in Monica and Lane than they were in her. Even when they told her otherwise. Even after months together. That tiny flutter of worry that she was intruding on their marriage – that she was temporary and they were permanent – hadn't gone away now that they were living together. If anything, their new arrangement had only amplified the tiny voice in her head that warned her not to get too attached. Seeing how comfortable they were with one another all the time – the way they understood each other's habits, needs and wants in ways she couldn't – made her feel as if she was desperately running behind them trying to catch up. Their vacation wasn't the problem, but the topic seemed to stoke Kierra's fear that she would say or do or ask for something they didn't want to give; something that was just for them. She felt as if she was walking on eggshells and it was throwing her for a loop.

Monica gently covered Kierra's shoulders with her hands and turned her around slowly. When they were facing each other, Monica stared at her for a few long seconds. Kierra's eyes skittered away.

"Why do you think I don't want you?" She asked eventually.

And just like that Kierra lost the battle. Tears pooled in her eyes and fell down her cheeks. "I'm sorry," she said as she pulled her sleeves over her hands and began to wipe at her eyes.

Monica's thumbs joined Kierra's and she helped blot the fat tears from her cheeks. She dug her fingers gently into Kierra's hair and massaged her scalp.

"What's wrong, sweet girl?" She whispered. "What did I do?"

Kierra shook her head and wiped at her glassy eyes. "It's just… you and Lane have been together forever and you have your own thing."

"We do," Monica conceded.

"And I know I can't have that with you two, but I just…" She shook her head again, running out of words to express how she felt.

"Lane and I do have our own thing," Monica said, her voice expressing the air quotes she couldn't make while the pads of her fingers soothed Kierra. "Just like you and Lane have your own thing."

Kierra frowned up at her.

"I haven't made or gotten him coffee in over three years because he doesn't think anyone can get it right if you're not there. He spends hours of his life searching the internet for the perfect heels for you, because my occasional pumps don't give him what he needs. And the late-night cookies you two think I don't know about, that he's not supposed to have… those are just some of your things. We each have our own relationships. That's how this works. That's the only way this works."

Kierra's tongue darted out to lick her bottom lip as she thought through Monica's words. She guessed she could see what Monica was saying but she lifted her eyes to ask the important question, "Then what's our thing?"

Monica's soft smile seemed to Kierra like sunshine after rain. She felt as if she hadn't seen it in forever. Monica backed Kierra to the wall and slipped her hands from Kierra's hair. Her palms grazed down her neck and shoulders to rest over her breasts. Kierra moaned. Her bare nipples hardened as the soft jersey material of her dress rubbed over them. Monica stepped between her legs and began to whisper against her jaw. Kierra's eyes closed in ecstasy.

"Lane hates flan and rum. You don't. And no matter how

much he loves you, he'll never watch the trash reality TV you like." She licked along Kierra's bottom lip. Her hands reached the hem of Kierra's dress and began to lift it.

"But you do."

"I'll watch that garbage with you for hours if you want," Monica whispered. Kierra laughed. Monica bit Kierra's bottom lip softly, dragging the flesh through her teeth. Kierra shivered.

"So you aren't going to get tired of me?" Kierra mumbled awkwardly in a breathy moan as just the tips of Monica's fingers traced feather light circles along her inner thigh.

"Never. The three of us are as permanent as Lane and I were when we met you."

Kierra's eyes drifted open. "Just us?"

Monica's eyebrows lifted. "That depends."

"On?" Kierra whispered.

"On if we want it to be the three of us. Or if there's room for more. Is that what you were afraid of? Really? That we would get tired of you? That we would replace you?"

Kierra bit her bottom lip and averted her gaze.

Monica brushed her lips against Kierra's. "I'm not like you. I don't wear my heart on my sleeve."

"I know," Kierra said.

"And I'm not like Lane. I don't say the first and second things that come immediately to my mind."

They both smiled. "I know that too," Kierra said.

"So you should also know that I'll never lie to you. If you're worried, then tell me. If you have a question, then ask me. And if you want to know how bad I want you and need you-" Kierra's body shook on a moan as Monica's hand settled over her bare sex and she slipped a finger inside in a fluid motion. "All you have to do is stand too close to me and you'll know." She smiled against Kierra's lips.

Kierra spread her legs and nodded as Monica pumped her finger in and out of her.

"I kept my hands off of you for three years, I don't plan to do that anymore than is absolutely necessary in the near or the far," Monica stressed that word, "future."

"Oh my god," Kierra moaned when Monica settled the heel of her hand over her clit. "But," she swallowed and shuddered before she could start speaking again. "But the vacation?"

Monica smiled sadly, "I wanted to take you to Puerto Rico. But I didn't want you to go there if you wanted to go somewhere else."

"Are you fucking kidding me?" Kierra breathed as she pulled Monica's mouth to hers. The kiss was desperate and relieved and lustful. Monica pumped her finger faster and Kierra moaned into her mouth.

Monica moved her free arm around Kierra's waist and lifted so that Kierra could wrap her legs around her body and gratefully thrust her hips into Monica's hand. The room filled with their moans and then Kierra's sharp cry as her orgasm washed over her. She wrapped her arms around Monica's shoulders and collapsed with a happy smile on her face. Monica kissed along her jaw and chin and nose as she calmed down; her thumb still gently circling her clit. Soft spasms wracked Kierra's body as she floated back to Earth.

When Kierra could stand, Monica eased her to her feet and brought her hand to her mouth. Kierra groaned as Monica sucked her essence from her fingers and palm. Monica smiled as she backed away. "Get dressed or we're going to be late."

Kierra was swaddled in bliss and she smiled, "Sure thing, boss."

"Something casual," Monica said.

Kierra nodded.

"And please put on some underwear and a bra."

Kierra frowned even though her gaze was still fuzzy. "You're asking a lot of me right now."

Monica's voice was full of the smile Kierra couldn't quite see but she knew well, "I'm not asking."

Kierra shivered and licked her lips.

***

THEY WERE SITTING in the back of a town car heading across the Edinburgh city center. Nestled in a trendy stretch of the downtown shopping area was an upscale vegan restaurant ostensibly owned by a renowned Swedish chef, but the establishment was actually registered in the name of Elijah Moore's wife. According to reliable intel, Elijah frequently visited the restaurant when he was in town. Mason had tracked him and other high-ranking P14 members to the restaurant every day since they'd arrived in Edinburgh. So it made sense that he and Lane should show up there and see if they could catch the group's attention.

Mason focused on the time constraints they were under as he sank slowly into his cover. He turned to Lane on the other side of the car, "So what's the deal with you three?"

Lane smiled as if he'd been expecting this question. As if he'd been asked it before and more than once. He turned to Mason and raised an eyebrow, "You're gonna need to be more specific."

"Professionally."

"Kierra's our PA. She's gonna take the Critical Materials exam soon."

"And personally?"

"We're together," Lane said simply.

"That's all you're going to say about it?"

Lane shrugged, "There's nothing else to say."

Mason remembered why the black ops team often hated working with field agents. Speaking to them was like speaking another language. "I'm asking because I need to know if there are boundaries you all would like me not to cross."

Lane lifted his eyebrows in interest. "Why didn't you just say that then?"

"I thought it was pretty obvious," Mason breathed.

"It wasn't." Lane smirked but then his mouth turned down into a frown as his eyes shifted to the side. "But you're right. Monica and I have an understanding, but we haven't talked to Kierra yet. We may need to renegotiate our arrangement." His eyes shifted back to Mason. He smiled almost like a kid in a candy store, "We're still in the honeymoon phase." He winked.

Mason couldn't help but smile. He didn't know what that felt like. He didn't do relationships. And not just because of his job, although that was the excuse he always used when asked about it. Not that that happened much these days. "I'll keep it PG then," Mason said with a chuckle.

Lane frowned even as his heated gaze swept over Mason's body. "Shame."

Mason laughed.

Their car slowed and he sat up straight.

"Show time," he said. "Are you ready?"

Lane smiled, "I'm *always* ready."

Mason mirrored Lane's interested glare. "Yeah," he huffed. "I bet you are." The car stopped and their driver exited. Before he opened Lane's door, Mason added, "You let me know if you three have that talk while we're here."

Lane stood from the car with a laugh.

Something about Lane's accent and the husky sound of his laughter brought the sound of Tiya's voice suddenly into his head. But he shut it down. He had a job to do and daydreaming about the way she wrapped her Southern accent around words like "play" and "baby" and "cock" would only distract him. And he didn't have time to be distracted. He never did. Or more accurately, he never let himself have the time.

Their car had stopped in front of a narrow alley that

looked like it had come straight out of a European period movie. The alley was almost wide enough for three people to walk side-by-side together and the cobblestone street was uneven and slick with moisture from rain and melted snow. It was charming. A brief flash of a memory crossed Mason's mind.

"I've never been anywhere interesting," Tiya said. "Send me good stories from wherever you are. Take me with you, lovers."

Mason gulped and buried that memory just as Lane spoke.

"So, chances that Moore will be here?" He whispered.

Mason shrugged. "Forty percent maybe. He comes at different times each day. We could have missed him. Or he could come just as we're leaving. We'll have to play it by ear."

Lane turned to him and laughed, too loud. It was a good laugh; a deep, sexy rumble. Great distraction. "That's my strong suit," he said with a wink.

They walked down the alley slowly, pretending to study all of the small boutiques they passed until finally they arrived outside of Earth's Bounty. They pretended to consider the restaurant: looking left and right down the alley, Mason checked his watch, while Lane pored over the menu, surreptitiously eyeing the dining room.

There was a couple sitting at a table and a bored waitress typing quickly on her phone just inside the door. The place was practically empty.

"So what do you wanna do?" Lane asked. "This is your op. We could come back later?"

Mason considered it. They could come back later but they could have also just missed their opportunity to run into Elijah. He had the rest of his team working on the extraction plan, but he could send someone to check in at the small country home where Elijah was staying. It was a difficult location but if they could confirm if Moore was there or not, the deviation could be worth it. He was turning the options over in his head when Lane clapped a hand on his back and laughed again.

"Guess that's that," he said and pulled Mason toward him.

When their mouths touched Mason's eyes widened in shock. He was preparing for Lane's tongue. It never came.

"Target acquired," Lane whispered against his lips.

They pretended to kiss, their lips moving dryly together, as all of their attention shifted behind Mason's back. Lane could see, but Mason had to discern what was happening by sound. A car door closed. Steps on cobblestone. A person was speaking, but Mason couldn't hear what they were saying. And then the steps stopped.

"Excuse me," a voice said behind them. Mason knew that voice.

He and Lane pulled apart and turned around.

"Sorry about that," Lane said as they moved out of the doorway.

"No need to apologize," Elijah Moore said in a crisp American East Coast accent that Mason knew was an affectation to hide his Pennsylvania Dutch origins. "Are you considering the restaurant?"

Lane smiled, "Among other things." He reached over to run his thumb across the knot of Mason's tie.

Mason watched as Elijah smiled, his eyes tracking the movement.

"The food is wonderful," Elijah said.

"Is it?" Mason asked. He grabbed Lane's hand and pressed his lips to the tip of his thumb.

He could hear the lust in Moore's voice. "Come," he said. "Please. As my guests. Let me show you."

"Is this your restaurant?" Lane asked.

Elijah chuckled. "You could say that."

Mason and Lane looked at each other, pretending to consider the invitation. They turned to Elijah, smiled and then followed the target into the restaurant. Mason placed a sure hand on Lane's shoulder and squeezed. He'd been tracking Elijah Moore for two months and in two minutes, Lane had gotten him a seat at his table. His superiors hadn't loved when he'd asked for their backup – lots of black ops agents thought they were an island and could always get their jobs done without field agent assistance. But Mason knew then – and was even more sure now – that his request for Monica and Lane's help had been the right call.

---

four

Kierra tried not to shiver as the wind nearly toppled her over. She clutched her coat closed at the neck and frowned.

"This is why you needed to change," Monica said, without looking at her.

"You could have just said that."

"I did. We're in Scotland in late December. Underwear was at least a given."

"I have on underwear, okay. We can stop harping on it."

Monica chuckled and turned suddenly to push Kierra back against the wall behind her. Kierra yelped. It was freezing out and was probably going to snow soon, but Monica's mouth was warm against hers. Kierra smiled as she parted her lips, humming around Monica's tongue. Monica unzipped her coat and for a second, the freezing wind made her shudder, but then she wrapped her arms around Kierra's waist and pulled her close. Kierra lifted her arms around Monica's shoulders and held her tight. The kiss ended when Monica sucked Kierra's bottom lip into her mouth and let it leisurely slip through her lips.

"Maybe I should wear underwear more often," Kierra said, breathless.

"Not on my account," Monica said. "Now look over my right shoulder. What do you see?"

It took a few seconds for Kierra's brain to clear and her eyes to focus. But when she could concentrate, she saw the trendy sign above Earth's Bounty's front door.

"Can you see inside?"

Kierra shook her head, "Windows are fogged. It's much warmer in there than out here." Then she turned to Monica. "Are Lane and Carlisle here yet?"

Monica shrugged. "They might be."

"Shouldn't we check? All four of us shouldn't be in the same place, right? You always say it's a rookie mistake to shove too many agents in together until it's time to take the target down."

Monica smiled down at her, "So you do listen to me?"

Kierra stretched up to kiss Monica's chin. But Monica moved and captured her mouth, kissing her deep and slow. Kierra knew that this kiss wasn't about their cover. It was Monica's way of trying to soothe Kierra after their encounter at the hotel. If she'd asked, Kierra would have told her that the orgasm took care of that. But she didn't ask, so Kierra scraped her teeth along Monica's tongue with a smile.

Monica pulled back and rested her forehead against Kierra's. "Normally I agree that we shouldn't have four agents-"

"Three agents and a PA," Kierra corrected.

"We shouldn't have so many people in one location," Monica continued as if she hadn't been interrupted. "But we're on a tight schedule. Besides, we're not here for Elijah Moore. We're here for his wife," Monica breathed the words against Kierra's jaw.

"Christine Logan," Kierra said, recalling her name from the dossier.

"She's not technically in the group's leadership. And there's no evidence that she's ever participated in any terrorist acts. She wouldn't even be on our radar if she weren't married to Moore."

"So what's the plan, boss," Kierra whispered.

"Simple. We need to grab Christine's attention so that Lane and Carlisle have a clearer path to Elijah."

Kierra lifted onto the balls of her feet to press another kiss to Monica's mouth. "Got it." And then she laughed, "Honestly, I thought this was going to be hard."

Monica started to shake her head but gasped as Kierra stepped to the right, out of her arms.

"Excuse me," she called across the small alley.

Monica whipped around and standing in front of the restaurant was Christine Moore, née Logan, smiling confusedly at them.

"Hi, ma'am," Kierra continued. "Is this where the queer ladies' tea is going to be?"

"The what?" Christine and Monica said at the same time.

Kierra walked across the cobblestone street with a bright smile on her face. She pulled her knit cap down to cover her ears. "The Queer Ladies Who Lunch, Edinburgh chapter. We heard about it from a Swedish backpacker we met in Berlin named Alice. She told us that if we were in town for New Year's Eve, we should drop by the lunch and meet people. I could have sworn it was supposed to be around here somewhere."

Christine frowned. Kierra watched as her confusion turned to interest, raking over Kierra's breasts in her light cashmere sweater. She saw the moment when Christine decided that whatever suspicion made her step out of her restaurant to see about the people huddled across the alley was less important than how great Kierra's breasts looked under her thin sweater, even with a bra. She was going to make sure she told Maya that when they were back home.

"I-I'm sorry. I've never heard of the Queer Ladies…"

"Queer Ladies Who Lunch. Edinburgh chapter. Or

maybe," she turned to Monica and frowned. "Maybe it was Glasgow?"

Monica recovered and walked to her. "Could have been, I guess."

Kierra sighed. "Well damn, I guess our New Year's Eve plans are a bust." She frowned for a second more but then smiled a good dirty smile at Monica, one that Lane would have appreciated. "Guess we'll have to spend the night in our hotel, eating vegan curry and licking champagne off of each other," she said with a nonchalant shrug.

Monica spluttered, like actually spluttered. Wait 'til Lane hears about this, she thought to herself.

"Wait," Christine said, near frantic.

They both turned to her. "We don't..." She licked her lips and her eyes darted down either side of the alley. "I don't know what the Queer Ladies Who Lunch is, I'm sorry. But if you're vegan, you're more than welcome to eat here." She licked her lips again and stepped forward. "And if you're looking for New Year's plans with friends," she reached out to twirl a finger in one of Kierra's curls, "I might be able to help with that as well."

Kierra licked her lips, Christine's eyes hungrily drinking in the sight. She turned to Monica and smiled, "See, I told you I'd find us someone, I mean, something to do." Christine's breath hitched. Kierra winked at Monica as Christine ushered them eagerly into the restaurant.

▭

MONICA'S WHISPER made her shiver. "Stop staring at them."

Kierra turned to her and reached out to stroke her face. "I can't help it. They look..." She wrinkled her nose and shook her head, searching for words. "They look cute together."

Lane and Carlisle were sitting across the dining room at

Earth's Bounty, at a table nearest to the kitchen. The restaurant was nearly empty, and Kierra had an unobstructed view of them as they smiled and laughed, and Carlisle wiped a bit of sauce from the corner of Lane's mouth and then licked it from his finger. Kierra knew she shouldn't be staring at them. It was like spy 101. And yet... she couldn't tear her eyes away.

Monica grabbed Kierra's chin, leaned across the table and pressed their mouths together, whispering only loud enough for Kierra to hear, "It's acting."

Kierra rolled her eyes and kissed Monica for real. She sat back in her chair and shrugged, "Yeah, I know that. I'm just saying. They're real cute together."

"Is there something we should discuss?"

Kierra's eyes flitted to Lane and Carlisle again. She licked her lips. "Not yet," she said, finally tearing her eyes away. She grabbed Monica's hands and smiled. "But soon. Maybe."

Monica lifted one of Kierra's hands to her mouth and brushed her lips across her knuckles. The slight kiss seemed to answer that she looked forward to it.

"Okay," Christine said, interrupting their quiet moment. "This mushroom bourguignon is nice and filling and will give you lots of energy for... whatever comes next." She placed a plate in front of Monica and another in front of Kierra. A waiter placed a seat at the head of their table and Christine sank into it with a smile.

"And what about mine?" Kierra asked with her best smile.

Christine leaned toward her, pointing with her index finger. "Our split pea soup with tempeh croutons is famous. It's also my favorite." Christine ran her finger across the back of Kierra's hand.

Kierra noticed the barest tensing of Monica's hands in her peripheral vision.

Someone cleared their throat. "Sweetheart," a male voice said.

They all turned to find Elijah Moore standing there, watching them.

Kierra wasn't entirely sure, but she thought she heard an irritated grunt come from Christine's direction.

"Oh sweetheart," Christine finally replied, standing from her seat. They leaned into a dry peck of a kiss that made Kierra sad before turning back to their table. When Elijah Moore laid eyes on Kierra and Monica his gaze wasn't as guarded as his wife's had been at first. The hunger Kierra saw there was possessive and wild and she had to force herself not to shudder in discomfort or suck her teeth in disgust.

"Hello, my name is Elijah," he said, reaching a hand out to Monica. He shook their hands, doing that gross thing that men often do where they cover one of a woman's hands with both of theirs so that they can grope at her skin that much more.

Kierra smiled but it felt hollow, because it was.

"Sweetheart, this is Luna and Rachel. They're here on vacation," Christine said.

Elijah smiled, "And you've chosen to spend some of your time with us? I'm delighted."

Christine pressed herself into Elijah's side and smiled at Kierra predatorily. "Aren't they lovely?" She whispered, almost to herself.

Elijah bared his teeth, "Yes. They are."

"And what about you?" Christine whispered, turning to look across the dining room toward Lane and Carlisle.

They all turned, and Kierra leaned around Christine, taking the opportunity to look her fill at them again. Lane and Carlisle were speaking to one another, their heads bent close. They feigned a slow recognition that they were being watched. Their heads turned and they smiled.

Elijah's voice sounded thick with desire when he spoke, "I found them outside kissing. Considering the menu. I couldn't help but invite them inside."

"Oh, how odd. Luna and Rachel were outside kissing as well," Christine said.

Monica reached for Kierra's hand. "There must be something about your restaurant," she said in the tone of voice – deep and intimate – that always felt like electricity over Kierra's skin. She squeaked a moan and whatever connection Christine was about to make drifted away as she watched Monica's thumb stroke Kierra's palm.

Across the restaurant, Lane grabbed his glass of wine and lifted it toward them. Carlisle leaned into his side, turned his head and his mouth almost brushed Lane's jaw. It was close enough that anyone watching might have assumed that their skin had touched, but Kierra was a hawk and her eyes zeroed in; close, but not quite. Still, it made her heart beat faster.

"I should get back over there," Elijah said. His voice sounded as if he'd already left them to head back to the other table.

Christine turned to her husband, "I just realized," she started. Kierra heard the false note in her tone. "I was thinking, dear. Luna and Rachel don't have New Year's Eve plans. What do you think about inviting them to our get-together tonight?"

Elijah stared blankly at her for a second, his attention still focused across the restaurant. But then he turned to Monica, his gaze heating.

"And your friends," Christine added. "I'm sure there's enough room for them as well."

That was all it took. The heat in Elijah's eyes seemed to intensify. He turned back to Lane and Carlisle. Kierra didn't want to notice his very obvious erection, but she did.

"That is an absolutely wonderful idea," Elijah said.

"What do you say?"

Monica lifted an eyebrow, "What kind of a get-together are you having?"

"Oh, it won't be as hectic as the city street party," Christine said with a chuckle. "Warmer for sure."

"We like to spend the evening in with a few friends…" He reached out to brush his hand over Monica's shoulder, "New and old alike. We believe it's important to enter the new year strengthening our… connections."

Christine purred.

Kierra wasn't sure if they were trying to be coy or if they didn't want to be overheard by their staff and other customers, but she could read between the lines: orgy. "Sounds like our kind of get-together," she purred back, running her hand up Monica's forearm.

"Lovely," Elijah said, putting an arm around his wife. "Then I'll go and extend an invitation to Peter and John. This might be our *best* New Year's Eve yet."

Kierra had to bite her lips shut. She had no doubt that Lane had chosen the cover names for this mission, because of course.

Kierra noticed only the briefest stiffening of Christine's lips before she followed her husband across the room, with an apologetic smile to them over her shoulder. She and Monica watched them pose the invitation to the men. They knew what the answer would be, but Kierra wanted just another reason to watch them again. And she was rewarded for being nosy. Everything in the room besides Monica's hand in hers fell away as Kierra drank in the moment Lane's hand smoothed over Carlisle's chest, slid down his abdomen and under the table. She gasped, imagining that his hand settled onto the other man's belt buckle. She had to force herself not to bounce excitedly in her seat. Monica squeezed her hand to bring her back to herself.

"We definitely need to talk," Monica mumbled.

Kierra tore her eyes away with a nod and licked her lips, "Yes please."

Thankfully Monica was a better spy than Kierra could ever pretend to be. The slight tensing of her jaw was barely noticeable. But the heat in her eyes… Well, that fit their cover, so it was okay, Kierra guessed as she rubbed her thighs together.

▭

LANE LIKED WATCHING Monica and Kierra, he always had. From that very first moment they'd all met, he'd found a thrilling pleasure in watching Kierra get underneath Monica's skin because it got under his. Monica was always so serious and focused. He loved that about her even as he realized that it was unsustainable. He'd known the first time he saw her that she would be the kind of woman who needed someone to help her let her hair down. It took him years and so much patience to figure out how to be that for her. And it was nice sometimes to be able to share that job with someone else. Hell, what took him time and effort came to Kierra as easy as breathing, and bit by bit he relinquished just a bit more of that responsibility to her so that he could sit back and enjoy the fruits of her labor: Monica's smile, her unexpected laugh, her gruff voice, breathy and labored, her high-pitched moans.

"You shouldn't be staring at them," Carlisle whispered.

"I'm not staring," he said, shifting his eyes to the other man with a smile. "I'm admiring."

Carlisle raised an eyebrow at him, "I don't know that I'm a man who likes his *husband* admiring strange women."

Lane slid his arm around Carlisle's back to rest on the back of his chair, but his palm pressed against his back. Just a light presence. "You are if I married you."

"Was that the stipulation?" His head inclined to the left toward Monica and Kierra's table.

Lane smiled, "Not in the way you're insinuating."

"What am I insinuating?" Carlisle asked, turning toward him, their thighs brushing.

"That one of us told the other person that we had to have

37

an open marriage. That's not who we are."

"Who are you? That's the question everyone at The Agency wants to know, by the way," Carlisle said, his head tilting forward.

Lane chuckled. "I bet." His eyes drifted to Monica again. She and Kierra were leaning toward each other over their plates. Smiling. "Did you go to college?" He asked Carlisle.

"I did."

Lane turned to him and squinted his eyes. "Were you as serious then as all you black ops dicks seem to be now?"

Carlisle smiled and shook his head. "Not even."

"Yeah, I thought so." He leaned just a bit forward toward him. "Do you remember what it was like to feel free? That first time you realized that you could make your own decisions and," he chuckled, "you made all the wrong ones?"

Carlisle's smile slipped only a fraction and he nodded.

"Do you remember the moment when you realized that you wanted something enough to get your shit together?"

Carlisle nodded again.

"I had all those moments with Monica. She was the thing I wanted enough to get my shit together. And I was the thing she wanted enough to give herself permission to live a little."

"So you grew up together?"

Lane nodded. "We did. And we promised never to smother any parts of ourselves to do it. That was the stipulation that we gave each other: that we would grow fully and wholly together."

"And that meant an open marriage?"

Lane shrugged, "For us, yes."

"And you don't get jealous?" Carlisle asked. He turned to look at the table across the dining room.

Kierra and Monica were kissing, gentle, innocent pecks of the lips. Kierra whispered something to Monica, and she pulled away from their kiss to laugh. Kierra's eyes lit up as she watched her. Lane's eyes lit up as he watched them.

"Of course we get jealous. We have in the past and we might in the future." He turned back to Carlisle. "But not about Kierra. If that's what you're asking."

Carlisle seemed to think about that before nodding.

"Every relationship is different. For Monica and me, we do everything and everyone," he said with a wink, "as a team. We've always wanted to experience everything together. What we like and don't like, what we need, what scares us, what makes us happy. We've built an entire relationship on trial and error. Together. And then we met Kierra."

"What changed?"

Lane turned back and his gaze settled on her, "Nothing. It wasn't that we both wanted her. Or even that she wanted us. We'd had that before. It was that we all needed each other. From the moment we met her she fit, like she was always supposed to be there. All that trial and error so that we would be able to recognize her when she walked into our lives."

"I don't know what that's like," Carlisle admitted.

Lane turned to him and frowned, "I'm sorry. This can be a terrible job if you're lonely." Lane lifted his left hand from Carlisle's back and settled it onto the other man's shoulder. He squeezed. "Are you lonely?"

Carlisle pressed his lips shut as he seemed to consider the question. And then his eyes flitted up over Lane's head. He knew by the way the other man's jaw ticked that someone was behind him. Lane moved his hand from Carlisle's shoulder, up his neck and gently stroked his cheek. Carlisle closed his eyes and Lane saw what he had probably been trying to decide if he wanted to share; all that loneliness and deprivation washed out his features. He wondered how long it had been since someone had touched him like this. If he had ever been touched like this.

"Is there anything else we can get for you?" Elijah said.

Lane took a second before he turned to smile at the other man. He was leaning on a chair across from them. His eyes were focused on Lane's hand on Carlisle's neck. He looked hungry. Greedy. They could work with that.

"No, thank you," Carlisle said, his voice hoarse.

"I think we're going to leave. Go back to our hotel to… rest before tonight," Lane added. He saw the widening of Elijah's eyes and his nostrils flare. Lane moved his thumb across Carlisle's cheek and skimmed it across his lips. Carlisle's mouth opened and his tongue gently swiped the pad of Lane's finger.

Elijah gasped.

"We're looking forward to tonight," Lane added.

Elijah was too overcome with lust to do anything but nod. Yeah, they could definitely work with that.

THEY HAD hours before the party. Mason and Lane left the restaurant before Monica and Kierra. They went back to his hotel room to go over their plan for tonight before Lane headed back to his own hotel room to fill in his wife and their assistant. Normally Mason would have tried to get a bit of sleep or gone over the plan a few dozen times. But after Lane left, he'd turned on an episode of Bawdy Boudoir. He took his phone into the bathroom, turned the volume all the way up and turned on the shower. He rolled his shoulders and waited for the water to heat. He could feel the stress he'd managed to ignore while they'd been undercover seep into his suddenly aching muscles.

"We have a letter from my fave, Jarhead," Tiya announced with a giggle. His dick jumped at the sound. "I can't wait," she whispered, as if she hadn't already read the story. As if she really savored his emails. He hoped.

"He says,

Dear Love-

I haven't written in a while. I've been traveling again so I have a new story for you. I hope you like it.
I was sitting in a café one night in Paris and I saw this couple. I thought they were husband and wife and they hated each other. I sat there for half an hour watching them, saddened. I don't know why. Maybe because they looked so disconnected, so alone even though they were together. That resonated with me. And I couldn't look away.
For almost an hour, they never spoke to each other. Not one word. But then, just as the sun set, the woman moved her hand to the man's pants. She pulled his dick from his open zipper and stroked him while she drank a glass of wine, leisurely. Elegantly, until he came in a mess over his lap. She wiped her hand on her napkin, drank the last gulp of wine in her glass, got up and left. Just like that. No words. No kiss goodbye. Just put her purse onto her shoulder and walked away.
I don't know what that was, but it wasn't a marriage. If it was, more people would probably stay married, don't you think?"

MASON WAS in the shower by the time Tiya was done reading his email. He had already covered his hand in expensive body wash and was stroking his dick slowly, his breath ragged. Listening to Tiya speak could rev him up even when she was reading the tamest stories. But listening to her read his story — his fantasy, really, of what he wanted to do with her — bowed his back in no time. Her soft moan after that last sentence made his balls ache.

"If you're new to the Bawdy Boudoir, I think you have a good idea why Jarhead has a special place in my heart now. This might be TMI, but his emails always make me wet."

Mason's hand moved faster over his dick and he groaned.

"Jarhead," Tiya said in a sultry voice. It sounded like she

was leaning close to the mic. "Wherever you are, I want you to know that I'll be thinking of you tonight when I touch myself."

Mason came in a forceful gush all over his hand, Tiya's name on his lips.

<hr>

LANE LET himself into their hotel room. The lights were off. It was quiet until he heard the moan. It was actually two mingled moans that harmonized perfectly as they fell past his favorite lips at the same time. He toed his shoes off and loosened his tie. He took his cufflinks off and slipped them into his jacket pocket before stripping it off his shoulders. He threw it haphazardly over the back of the couch. He'd unbuckled his belt and was unbuttoning his shirt when he pushed the bedroom door open to the darkened room.

Monica was on top of Kierra. Her legs were wrapped around Monica's waist. Monica's hips moved in a rhythmic and gentle rotation. Lane didn't need the lights to see Monica's harness. Their mouths were so close; flashes of their tongues made a slight sheen of sweat break out on his forehead. Lane only realized that Monica was whispering to her, when Kierra answered with a moaned "yes" that made his dick painfully hard and his balls feel heavy in his underwear.

Monica's voice rose. She knew he was there.

"Do you want him?" Monica asked.

"Yes," Kierra moaned again.

Lane smiled and began to walk toward the bed.

"Do you want Lane to fuck him?"

Lane's steps faltered and his hands stilled on the button of his slacks.

"I want you to fuck me while Lane fucks him," Kierra said, her voice shaky and dripping with lust.

"Who's him?" He asked.

Kierra's head fell back as Monica increased the speed of her thrusts. Their moans filled the room. Monica licked the column of her neck and Lane nearly ripped his pants open, the need to touch them, be inside one of them as quickly as possible making his hands shake. He was naked in a heartbeat. "Who's him?" He asked again as he crawled onto the bed.

Monica finally turned to him, their eyes locked as she ground her hips into Kierra. Lane grasped his shaft and began to pump.

"Carlisle," Monica finally said. Kierra moaned. "She got wet watching you with Carlisle."

Lane laughed, moved to the head of the bed and brushed his hand over the crown of Kierra's head. She was in bliss. He wasn't sure if she heard him. "It's just the mission, sweet girl."

"It doesn't have to be," Monica said.

Lane turned to her and smiled. "He asked about our boundaries."

Monica was watching him. She stopped fucking Kierra momentarily and sat up on her knees. She grabbed Kierra's hips to hold her in place. Kierra squirmed, begging in soft moans until Monica started to stroke into her again; this time in shallow but hard thrusts.

Lane felt the shiver ripple through Kierra's body from her core outward.

"*Our* boundaries?" Monica said.

Lane gently cupped Kierra's chin and turned her head. He kept his eyes on Monica and touched the head of his dick to Kierra's lips. She moaned. He shivered as her tongue and warm, wet mouth engulfed him, stroking his length with firm suction.

"Our boundaries," Lane repeated.

He caught a glimpse of Monica's smile before she turned her attention back to Kierra. She began to grind into her again. The errant rays of the setting sun bounced off of their sweaty bodies. He took comfort in the fact that he was home.

five

Just as Mason stepped out of the shower there was a knock on his hotel room door. He wrapped a towel around his waist, grabbed his firearm and called out, "Who is it?"

"The concierge, sir. I have a message for you." Mason recognized that voice.

He looked through the peephole and recognized the man on the other side of the door. Sanchez was his number two in the field. Mason trusted him with his life, and he was his designated go-between. If he needed a message while he was undercover, his only trusted source was Sanchez. This was an expected relay.

He pulled the door open. Mason's wet hair was dripping into his face and his colleague's eyes raked over his bare chest with a smile. "You had a message from your employer while you were out, sir," he said in a passable Glaswegian accent. He extended his arm to hand Mason an envelope.

Mason grabbed it and smiled. "Thank you."

"You're welcome... sir," Sanchez replied, turned, and walked away.

Mason closed the door and walked backward into the sitting room, his eyes on the door just in case. He opened the envelope with one hand, the other still gripping his gun – because he could never be too prepared, not even with Sanchez. The card he pulled from the envelope had a series of numbers handwritten on it confirming the extraction details. Mason recognized the coordinates for the Moores's cottage and a time. Everything looked in order, so he headed back into the bathroom. He dropped the card onto the bathroom counter by his cell phone. He put his gun next to the card and queued up another episode of Bawdy Boudoir. This one was a few weeks old, but it was one of his favorites.

"Hello lovers," Tiya said in the husky voice she always used for her greeting. "Have I got a treat for you. I've been writing again." She sounded so happy that it made him smile, every time. "Each week you all send me the sexiest stories. And when I was going through my dry spell, the submissions doubled. So I thought I'd start today's episode with a few words of my own. As a thank you."

There was an awkward moment of silence. He held his breath and waited for his favorite part of this story: her soft moan. He wondered how she wrote that out. He wondered how that moan would sound directly in his ear. He wondered if he would ever get to hear it. He shook his head knowing that was never going to happen because if it did, something had gone seriously wrong. That's what he had to remind himself to keep his desperation for her at bay. If he ever got that close to Tiya Randall, her life would be in danger and it would be all his fault.

—

"NOW THIS IS MUCH BETTER," Kierra said as she smoothed her hands over the floor-length purple velvet slip dress she'd bought for Christmas. She hadn't gotten a chance to wear it since they'd technically spent the entire day either naked underneath their robes or just naked. It was the best

Christmas Kierra had ever had and was absolutely worth the very long, passive-aggressive voicemail her aunt had left when she'd told her she wasn't coming home. But she had wished she'd gotten the chance to wear the dress. Even for a little while.

She gathered her hair at the top of her head, "You think I should wear my hair up?"

Lane slipped his shirt onto his body and moved to stand behind her. He kissed her at the base of her neck.

She shivered. "Definitely up," she decided.

He tilted his head to lock eyes with her in the mirror. He wrapped his arms around her waist. "Have you decided where you want to go for our vacation?"

She smiled just as she saw Monica move into their room in her peripheral vision. Kierra nodded, "Puerto Rico." She watched Monica's steps falter. Lane leaned down to kiss Kierra on her pulse. She could feel the smile on his mouth.

"As soon as we're done here," he said loud enough for Monica to hear.

Kierra leaned back into him. Monica moved closer to them, the warmth from her body at their left. Kierra locked eyes with her in the mirror. She smiled at the softness she saw there. It wasn't new, but on a mission Monica could be guarded; shut down so that she could do what needed to be done. And even if it wasn't the best idea, Kierra always loved being able to get under her skin and remind her to be soft, just for them, no matter how dangerous the world outside their bubble might be.

Monica moved in front of Kierra, her voice thick with emotion when she spoke. "And what about Carlisle?"

Kierra licked her lips and ground her ass back into Lane's groin. "What would you have done before me?"

Lane scraped his teeth along Kierra's neck, just where it joined her shoulder. "If he wanted us and we wanted him…" His words trailed off and he licked at her skin.

"Like with me?" Kierra asked in a breathy voice as her nipples began to harden.

Monica's hand moved up Kierra's body. She pushed one of the straps of her dress off of her shoulder. Her index finger traced across Kierra's collarbone, down to the top of her breast and she pulled the dress farther down to bare her nipple; she circled it with her thumb. "We've never had anyone like you," Monica whispered.

"And we don't need anyone else," Lane added quickly. "It could be just the three of us from here on out." He laughed. "Lord knows you're a handful."

Kierra groaned as he flattened his hands onto her stomach and pulled her back into his growing bulge. Monica grasped Kierra's breast at the same time, the firm sharpness of her hand turning that groan into a sharp hiss. They often worked in tandem on her.

"The perfect handful," Monica breathed.

Monica moved in front of her and pushed the other strap over Kierra's shoulder. The only thing stopping her from climbing into Monica's arms again was Lane's firm hold on her. It was frustrating and exhilarating.

"Please," Kierra begged as Monica's thumbs softly circled her nipples.

"We don't need anyone else," Lane said again.

Kierra tipped her head back to his shoulder on a soft moan. She licked her lips and watched Monica's face. Her expression was almost flat, but Kierra knew the small signs of strain; squinting eyes, tight lips. She smiled.

"You two are mine," she said, rubbing her thighs together. "I'm possessive, but not selfish."

Monica licked her lips and pinched her nipples. Kierra groaned.

"Tell us what you want," Monica said in a harsh voice, another sign that she was reaching her limit.

"If he's open," Kierra said, reaching out to grasp Monica's waist. "And you're open." She scraped her nails down the bare skin of Monica's hips. "I want Agent Carlisle in our bed when the mission is over."

"Just him?" Lane said.

"For now," Kierra said. "But if we like it, I wouldn't mind sharing you two. Sometimes." She stressed that last word.

Monica nodded once and then her face flashed with relief as she lowered her head to suck one nipple into her mouth.

"And if he's not interested?" Lane asked, unconsciously grinding his dick into her ass.

Kierra moaned. Her words were stilted, thick with desire. "I don't think we'll have a hard time finding someone else." She reached around her body and gripped his dick. She could have orgasmed right there when he moaned into her ear and Monica scraped her teeth along her nipple. But she held herself together, anticipating all that was to come.

MASON DROPPED into the same chair he'd sat in before with a smirk. He wasn't sure if they were trying to hide the fact that they'd just fucked; if they were, they were failing. Terribly. Not that they had a reason to hide it since the gossip about Monica and Lane's exploits were legendary *before* they'd started dating their PA. Since then... well, their names were on everyone's lips. Even the black ops crew knew about them, which was saying something. But gossip was one thing. Walking into their post-orgasmic bliss was another thing altogether.

They were sitting on the couch, Kierra sandwiched between the other two, curled into Monica's side. Lane had thrown his arm over the back of the couch, one of his fingers twirling in the dark curtain of Monica's hair. Mason didn't usually have time for sex while on the job. The black ops division was nothing like the deep cover work Monica and Lane normally did. When he got too horny in the field, he usually eased the tension with a few episodes of the Bawdy Boudoir, a bottle of lube and his hand. But as he sat across from them, his skin felt hot and tingly. How long since he'd been with someone besides a disembodied voice?

And as if she knew what he was feeling, a slow smile spread across Kierra's mouth.

Mason shifted in his chair and leaned forward, his hands on his knees to hopefully hide the growing bulge in his lap. He got to the issue at hand. "Here's how I want to run this. I've got an exfil team that'll be ready to smuggle Moore out of the country once we have him in custody."

"Just Elijah?"

Mason nodded, "We've been following them both and while we know Christine's involved in the organization, we can't pin any of the bombings to her. None of the bombers ever mention her and Elijah is absolutely the figurehead. So our orders for tonight are to take him only. But anyone who gets in the way either comes with us or we take them down."

Lane shrugged, "It's your mission."

"What do you need us to do?" Monica asked.

"Christine seems interested in you two," he said, looking directly at Kierra.

"Can you blame her?" She said as she brushed a kiss along Monica's jaw.

Mason's eyes widened and he looked to Monica and then Lane. Monica's face was blank as if she wasn't at all affected by Kierra's actions. Lane smiled lazily back at him and moved a hand to rest on Kierra's hip.

Mason cleared his throat, shook his head and laughed. "I guess I can't." He took a deep breath to settle his nerves. It didn't quite work, but he felt comfortable continuing. "If you two can keep her distracted while Lane and I lure Elijah away, we can be in and out of there before you know it."

"And then what?" Kierra asked.

Mason opened and closed his mouth. Lane's smiled widened.

"What do you mean?" Mason asked.

"She means, if we're in and out before we know it, what will we do for the rest of the night? It is New Year's Eve after all," Monica said. It was the most matter-of-fact proposition he'd ever received. And oddly, it worked for him.

Mason's eyes shifted to Lane, "So I guess you three talked about your boundaries?"

Lane smiled smugly and shrugged, "We did. And apparently, we don't have many."

"What about you?" Monica asked.

Mason's eyes shifted to her and there was something about her hard glare that sucked him in. It was a few seconds before he answered. "Me?"

Mason's eyes followed the movement of her hand as it met Lane's on Kierra's hip. He was staring at their twined fingers when she asked again. "What are your boundaries?"

He let out a shaky breath. And then he heard Tiya's voice in his head, *"Don't you want to try something new, lovers? Isn't it time you stopped telling yourself no?"*

He nodded his head absently at her voice in his head. "As it happens, I don't have many boundaries either. And I've been on mission for a while," he said. What he didn't say was that he only had one boundary that mattered, and it was keeping him from the one thing he wanted above everything else.

"This is going to be so much fun," Kierra exclaimed, pulling Mason out of his own head. He smiled and tasted the new sensation of having something to look forward to. Instead of hopping on a plane to a new location, another job and another lonely night in a hotel room with his hand, her voice and his unfulfilled desires.

six

As often happened, when Mason entered a building connected to a surveillance subject, he had a few moments of déjà vu where his brain overlaid the image of the building in front of him with the blueprints he'd studied. It was his way of looking for liabilities; walls where they shouldn't be, curious doors, a ceiling height that didn't make sense. It seemed small, but as he'd been taught – and quickly learned once he entered the field – simply paying attention to your surroundings could save your life. Or not.

As he and Lane walked together around the main sitting room, nodding obliquely at the people they passed, he was shocked to find that nothing seemed out of place. This wasn't even a particularly crowded party, which wasn't ideal, but they could make it work. They could especially use the fact that the house was choppy, many small rooms separated by walls and short hallways. Mason had confirmed almost as soon as they arrived that Sanchez had been right; their best extraction point would be the small mudroom off the kitchen at the back of the house. Mason didn't want to get ahead of himself, but it seemed as if this might be the fastest rendition of his career.

"Now comes the hard part," he whispered to Lane as they

made their way through the main living room to a smaller parlor.

"And that is?"

"Getting Elijah's attention and luring him to the back of the house."

Lane turned to him with a smirk on his face and a sympathetic gleam in his eyes. "They really don't teach you all how to use your natural gifts, do they? It's all weapons and explosives and misdirection?"

Mason frowned, "What do you mean?"

He tilted his head and turned away, gesturing for Mason to follow him. In a small, dark hallway between the parlor and the dining room, Lane stopped and turned to him. He put his hands on Mason's shoulders and pushed him gently back against the wall.

"This isn't the time," he said, his mouth going suddenly dry but his dick twitching in his pants.

Lane's hands moved up the column of his neck and he gripped his face, his fingers pressing gently at the base of Mason's head. It might have calmed him, if Mason was one to panic in the middle of an op. But he wasn't panicking, so the feeling of Lane's fingers pressing him there turned that twitching in his pants into a rush of electricity.

"What do they say about us at The Agency?" Lane asked.

"What?" Mason gasped as Lane moved forward and pressed their bodies together. Lane's next words caressed the soft shadow of a beard on Mason's face.

"About Kierra? What do they say about my wife and I always bringing our assistant into the field?"

Mason had been trained to keep a clear mind for up to three days against most kinds of torture, but his brain felt fuzzy in a way that he'd never been trained to resist. And to be honest, he didn't want to. "People think you're crazy and putting everyone you work with in danger. Because-" Lane's thigh moved between Mason's legs and pressed against his hardening dick. Mason swallowed thickly.

"Because," Lane prompted, their lips almost touching.

"Because she's untrained. She's just a civvie." Lane smiled against his lips and swept his tongue over the seam. Mason's mouth opened immediately. He wanted to taste him.

But Lane pulled away and tilted his head. "Come see how untrained she is."

Lane walked further down the hallway to another small sitting room. In the main living room, people were pretending that this was a regular New Year's Eve get-together. But in this back room, the heat had risen considerably, and the truth of the night's festivities were barely hidden under the veneer of casual party chatter. It didn't take long to realize what was different about this crowd.

Hidden in a far corner, Monica and Kierra were sitting on a small settee. At first glance they looked like two people having an intimate conversation, heads bent close. But if you looked for a few seconds longer, you might catch a flash of Kierra's tongue as it glided along the outer shell of Monica's ear or their lips brushing against each other's gently in passing. Their connection wasn't a surreptitious encounter; it was an extended seduction of each other, and the entire room around them. If one looked longer, harder, it would have been easy to become entranced, as Mason did, with the way Monica's hand smoothed up Kierra's bare shin, gripped her knee and then slid, ever so slowly – and without one second of hesitation no matter how loud the room around them got – under her dress and between her legs. Mason assumed that if he and Lane had been closer, they might have heard whatever sound Kierra made when her mouth fell open. Was it a gasp? Or a moan? Mason was desperate to know. But whatever sound she'd made had gotten the attention of every person close enough to hear it and that far end of the room went silent as their audience turned – some blatantly, some briefly – toward that dark corner and the women on the settee.

"The entire room is focused on her." Lane's breath tickled Mason's ear and his tall, lanky body settled behind him. He wrapped an arm around Mason's waist and pulled him back, grinding his bulge into Mason's ass.

"And your wife," Mason whispered.

Lane's chuckle sounded sexy in Mason's ear. "My wife hates the spotlight. She might have been black ops if it wasn't for me. But Kierra just has this way about her. She loves the attention."

The best part of his training had been learning how to process large amounts of information at once. It was the kind of thing that kept someone like him alive long enough to keep someone like Lane alive when he provided tactical support. But once again Mason felt as if he'd reached the limits of his training. Because it was all he could do to comprehend Lane's words, the small movements of Kierra's hips as Monica's hand moved under her dress, the intense eye contact and whispered conversation between the two women, and Lane's hand, as it moved down his front and cupped his dick in a firm grip.

Mason moaned. It had been so long since someone else had touched him this way.

"How does she do it?" Mason asked.

"Hmm," Lane breathed, his tongue circling Mason's earlobe.

Mason's hips jumped as Lane squeezed him. He was breathless when he spoke, "How does she get under her skin like that?"

"The same way I got under yours," Lane said. As he spoke, Monica and Kierra seemed to realize that they were there and turned.

Mason locked eyes on Kierra, whose mouth was open on a moan? Deep breaths? Mason didn't know and he hated not knowing. He watched as Monica kissed and bit Kierra's bare shoulder. She wrapped a hand behind Kierra's back and Mason watched as it appeared to grasp at Kierra's breast, her other hand pumping noticeably.

Mason's eyes flitted around the room. While most eyes were glued on the far corner, some had now turned to him and Lane. "How?" Mason asked, unable to reiterate his question fully as Kierra bit her bottom lip, her eyes fluttering closed as her orgasm neared. Lane slipped his hand into Mason's unzipped pants.

"I wanted to," Lane said, as if it was that simple.

It wasn't. Mason wanted to tell him that it was absolutely not that simple. That whatever the fuck he and Kierra were doing to capture the attention of the entire room was not something he'd ever been taught as a means of misdirection. But he couldn't find the words to tell Lane that because Kierra's hands tightened, one on the side of the settee and the other on Monica's thigh. Her head fell back on a moan, this time mercifully loud enough for Mason to hear. Her body shook with the force of her orgasm.

Lane's hand was a gentle pressure on his dick, but not enough to get him off. He wanted to tell him to stroke him, to pull him into their own corner or, even better, to walk across the room to that other corner. But there was some gaping pit in his chest that ached as he watched Monica kiss her way up Kierra's neck and use her nose to nudge her just under her chin. Kierra's smile as she lowered her head and kissed Monica deeply made Mason feel lonelier than he had in years. Even Lane's hand on his dick couldn't push that away.

Thankfully, Lane's body tensed, and he removed his hand from Mason's pants. "Incoming," he whispered into Mason's ear.

Mason kept his eyes on Kierra and Monica for a few seconds more before turning to the other entrance into the room. Elijah and Christine Moore stood staring at them. Elijah's eyes were hungry while Christine seemed vaguely amused until she spotted Monica and Kierra in their corner. Her eyes lit up and she walked quickly away from her husband without a word or a backwards glance.

Lane was right. Kierra might have been an untrained civilian, but he'd known field agents who needed weeks to do what Kierra had done in hours. Now that they'd effectively separated Christine from her husband, it was time to do what they'd come here for. Lane zipped Mason's pants up and patted his erection gently. The absurdity of it made Mason laugh unexpectedly. And Elijah, who'd been surveying the room and everyone he'd invited here, turned his head to look their way. He smiled at them. Mason was still smiling from his laughter and he forced himself not to let it fade. Lane grabbed his hand and led the way across the room.

"Good evening," Elijah said to them in that crisp accent.

"Good evening," Lane replied in a plain Midwestern accent.

"Are you enjoying yourselves?" Elijah asked.

Lane smiled, "It's not what we expected, but thank you for inviting us."

Elijah frowned, "What did you expect?"

Lane turned his head and drew their attention to the corner where Kierra was snuggled against Monica and they were laughing with Christine, her hand on Kierra's knee.

Mason was cool under fire and under cover. But there was a reason he'd wanted field agents to accompany him on this op rather than someone from his black ops team. Black ops agents effectively had two settings: look, but don't touch or smash and grab. This mission was supposed to be a long-term surveillance op, but Mason had been called in when it turned into an active and immediate rendition situation after a P14 bombing in Belgium. It took him two months of waiting for the right moment to present itself, waiting for the opening to become clear. But field agents – *these* three field agents in particular – hadn't needed to wait around. They'd created the opening and put all the chess pieces on the board precisely where they wanted them. It was the first time Mason had ever wished he'd declined the black ops invitation.

Elijah extended his hand to trace the collar of Lane's opened dress shirt. He turned to Mason and smiled that same feral smile from earlier in the day, "Have you been given a tour of the cottage?"

"No," Mason croaked.

Elijah smiled. "Would you like one?"

"That depends," Lane interjected.

Elijah's eyebrows raised, "On?"

"On if the tour ends at a bed." Lane's hand covered Elijah's on his chest and his smile was a dirty promise.

Elijah seemed at a loss for words. Mason was shocked at that. How had Lane so effectively silenced a man who was building a cult-like following so blind they'd been willing to kill other human beings for their cause? This was the kind of masterclass he'd needed as a young agent. And his shock only continued as Lane released Elijah's hand and grabbed Mason behind the back of the head. Their faces moved slowly, just slow enough, he realized, that Lane was giving him a way out. He could say no. He could assert this as a boundary.

His eyes caught just over Lane's shoulder on Kierra. She was watching them. As his mouth touched Lane's and their lips moved together, his eyes bored into Kierra's as he parted his lips and gently pushed his tongue into the other man's mouth. Kierra licked her lips and grinned, her fingers playing with the thin strap of her dress. The soft fabric at the deep neckline threatened to fall and expose even more of her silky flesh. Mason found himself desperate to see her dark nipples and taste them. He kissed Lane harder. It was a promise of what was to come.

▭

THE DISTANCE from the small parlor to the kitchen was just a few feet, but the walk seemed to take forever. Every few steps someone called from a room to say hello to Elijah, all of them looking up at him as if he were the second coming. It was disturbing to say the least. Mason used the discomfort he felt to push some of the lust clouding his brain aside so that he could focus on the task at hand. The Agency had sent him after Elijah Moore and Passage 14, because they needed to be stopped.

"Where are you going, Elijah?" a voice called from the library. A man appeared in the doorway, leveling his wary gaze at Mason and Lane. Mason recognized him from his surveillance as Elijah's devoted assistant and sometimes lover, Arnold Walsh. He was usually attached to Elijah at the hip. Mason had planned for this contingency. He would take Arnold down if he had to.

"I'm just giving our new… friends," Elijah said, turning to look at them. Lane squeezed Mason's shoulder and pressed into his body from behind. Elijah cleared his throat; his face reddening and he began again. "I'm giving our new friends a tour of the cottage."

"I can do that," Arnold said. "That's beneath you."

Mason could have laughed. Lane did chuckle softly.

"That's quite alright, Arnie," Elijah said, irritation and arousal making his voice rough.

Arnold's face fell and his shoulders slumped at the rebuke. Elijah stepped forward. Mason watched as he reached out and grasped Arnold's shoulders, pulling him into a hug. Arnold relaxed into the embrace, wrapping his arms around Elijah's body. Mason heard Elijah whisper softly to the other man. Whatever he said made the other man relax. When they stepped out of the embrace, Arnold's face had transformed from pinched and hurt to bright and open. No human being should have that kind of control over another, Mason thought to himself.

Lane squeezed his shoulder. Mason's body had tensed. He forced his muscles to relax and smiled. When Arnold looked back at them, he winked and whispered, "enjoy…" before he turned and walked away.

"Shall we?" Elijah asked, gesturing for them to follow him.

They were just outside of the kitchen. If they turned left at the end of the hallway, they would pass the front living room and reach a short flight of stairs leading upstairs. But if they turned right, they could cross the kitchen in a few steps, fling open the back door and the extraction team would be there. Mason was lifting his hands to grab Elijah from the back and wrap his arms around his neck until he passed out, when the kitchen door swung open. He settled his hands on Elijah's shoulders and squeezed. Mason felt the shiver run through Elijah's body.

"Oh, hello, Mr. Moore." Mason didn't recognize the young woman, but she was wearing a server's uniform.

"Hello," he said as he turned his head and brushed his mouth against Mason's hand.

Lane moved around them and wrapped an arm around the woman's shoulders, an alluring smile on his face. "Is Mrs. Moore in the kitchen?"

The woman's face flushed, and she shook her head. "N- no. There's… there's no one in there?"

Lane frowned. "Hmmm. Do you have any idea where she might be? We've been looking all around for her."

It was such a deft lie that Mason was impressed and lying was the crux of their job. But he didn't want Elijah to notice it, so he moved his index finger to lightly caress the man's face. It was a necessary distraction and it worked. As did Lane's.

"I- I can go find her for you," she offered eagerly.

"Would you mind?" Lane asked, laying it on a bit thick.

She shook her head and smiled up at him before hurrying away. They waited until she was out of sight before Lane turned and grabbed Elijah by the front of his pants, slipping his fingers into the waist of his slacks and pulling him forward, through the kitchen door.

It took Elijah a second to realize where they were. He shook his head. "Upstairs," he croaked.

Lane cut him off by pulling him forward and crushing their mouths together, still moving backward toward the door. Mason took the opportunity to pull his phone from his pocket and alert his team. He then opened his coat, pulled out the syringe hidden in his breast pocket and slipped the needle into Elijah's exposed neck.

He reared back in shock, his wide eyes moving between the two men. Shock turned to rage, and he was gearing up, they could both see, to rush them. That was always the first impulse for men like him; anger when things didn't go their way. And that worked in their favor. The rush of anger made the blood pump harder, pushing the drug through his system faster. Just as he was about to explode, the fire in his eyes died and he collapsed, crumpling to the floor.

"Let's tie him up," Lane said, pulling hand ties from his breast pocket and handing some to Mason. They almost had him completely secured when the kitchen door opened and the same young girl gasped, looking down on them. Mason could see the scream building in her throat, and it made him sad. Christine, he was prepared to take if he had to. Arnold, he would absolutely take. But this girl who he didn't even recognize… He hated when civilians got involved.

▭

MONICA WAS a deep reserve of patience. She was calm and levelheaded and focused. She was also seconds away from breaking every bone in Christine Moore's right hand, which had not moved from Kierra's knee since she'd joined them.

Bystanders probably couldn't see her rage, but she knew Kierra could feel it. But they both knew that right now they had no choice. So Kierra leaned closer against Monica's side and tried to reassure her that this would be over soon. But seconds soon and minutes soon and hours soon were very different temporal realities and Monica wasn't sure that any of those options would be soon enough.

They were waiting for the signal from Lane and Mason that they'd captured Elijah and the extraction team had him so they could make their excuses and leave. Or, because it always paid to be prepared, they were waiting for word that something had gone wrong and the two needed backup. But the seconds seemed to drag on for hours and still no word.

Relief of sorts came when a young girl slunk into the room, timid and shy. She whispered to Christine that her husband was looking for her. Christine seemed irritated at the intrusion.

"I don't interrupt him when he's busy," she hissed, her eyes settling on Kierra's chest.

Monica's fist clenched at Kierra's side. Kierra moved to soothe her fingers with a soft touch.

She wanted to stay. They needed her to stay. But Monica saw the moment when Christine decided to leave.

Kierra saw that as well. She moved a hand to cover Christine's on her knee – the hand Monica really wanted to fucking break – and sucked her bottom lip into her mouth. Christine was hypnotized.

"Tell my husband that I'm busy and I will find him later," she whispered, moving her free hand to Kierra's other knee, this one gripping, not just resting.

Monica decided to break that hand as well.

"Ma'am, are y-you sure?" The girl asked.

"Very," Christine whispered.

The girl looked confused and nervous.

Monica hated to do this, but it had to be done. She squeezed Kierra's side and turned to the girl. "Excuse me," she said, pulling her attention away from Christine. "Can you show me to the toilet?"

"Um," the girl said, her eyes shifting back to Christine momentarily.

"Look at me," she demanded.

She felt Kierra shiver against her; she did always love when Monica barked out orders.

The girl complied and swallowed.

"The bathroom," Monica said again.

She nodded and Monica stood. "I'll be back," she said to Kierra.

"We'll be here," Christine answered, never taking her eyes off of Kierra.

It was only Monica's self-control that kept her from flinging Christine across the room.

She followed the girl out of the parlor down a small hallway. Her hands were clenching at her sides. Just past the kitchen door, the girl gestured toward a small half-bathroom and Monica smiled at her in thanks. She walked into the room but didn't close the door completely.

She heard another door open and the young girl gasped. There was a beat of silence before a male voice, one she didn't recognize, called down the hall.

"Elijah?"

Monica peeked out of the door and saw a stocky man heading toward the kitchen. She held her breath as he pushed the kitchen door open. She moved slowly. He never even heard her coming.

⸻

"I'M REALLY SORRY ABOUT THIS," Lane breathed to the terrified girl. He had one hand covering her mouth as he held her around the waist.

"What do you want to do about her?" He asked Mason.

Mason secured the last restraint, hogtying Elijah for ease of transport, and looked up at Lane. "Knock her out. We're taking her with us. We have to go."

The girl's eyes widened, and she began to scream or plead, he couldn't quite hear with Lane's hand muffling her words.

"I'm not knocking her out," Lane said. He looked down at the girl and repeated the words to her reassuringly, "I'm not going to knock you out. I'm not that kind of man."

"Do your job, Agent," Mason commanded.

Field hierarchy was quite clear in The Agency; black ops agents had seniority. It didn't matter whose mission they were on or how many years the black ops team had, what they said was law, because their mission parameters were to save the agent and the operation and there was no margin for error. Field agents on the other hand often did exactly what Lane was doing: prioritizing civilians over the mission. It was altruistic, but The Agency was not a human rights organization. They had a job to do. Field agents and black ops were two sides of the same coin. Moral standards were great in the field until the job went belly up. When that happened, black ops agents were trained to dispel the kind of moral quandaries that might, for instance, make them want to leave behind an innocent waitress who just happened to stumble upon them kidnapping her boss. And Mason was about to remind Lane that he had the final word when the kitchen door swung open again.

Arnold's face was contorted with confusion and then rage as he took in the scene in front of him; his boss on the floor tied up like an animal and Lane restraining the server. Mason stood and wished he'd brought a firearm on this mission. But he didn't need it. Monica moved into the kitchen after Arnold, who was too focused on them to notice her behind him. She snatched a skillet from the stove as she passed and swiftly brought it down onto Arnold's head. They all watched as the man fell onto his boss in a heap.

There was a second of tense silence before the server began to squirm in Lane's arms.

"What's this?" Monica asked her husband.

"Collateral," Mason answered.

She turned to him and didn't frown, but Mason could feel the disapproval in her words. "We don't operate that way," she said simply.

Mason didn't even think of reminding her that he outranked her. He couldn't think of a black ops commander who would in that moment.

"What do you want to do?" Lane asked.

She turned her eyes to the girl and stared at her. "If he moves his hand, will you scream?"

She shook her head wildly, tears building in her eyes.

"Of course she would say that," Mason said.

Monica ignored him and peeled Lane's hand from her mouth. The server shook her head and pressed her lips together.

"What's your name?" Monica asked.

"Suzanne," she said, her Scottish accent thicker than it had been before. "Bu-but everyone calls me Suzy."

"Are you a member of Passage 14 or Coming Dawn, Suzy?"

She shook her head emphatically. "I'm just filling in for my sister to make some extra money."

"What do you need the money for, Suzy?"

"I," tears started streaming down her cheeks, "I met a bloke online. He lives in Brazil. I'm moving there. We're going to get married."

Monica smiled. "That's sweet." She grasped Suzy's shoulders as Lane slowly released her and backed away. "Suzy, I want you to listen to me." Suzy nodded. "We're going to take these two out of here. If anyone asks if you've seen them, all you have to do is say that you haven't. In two weeks, we'll transfer enough money into your account to buy a first-class ticket to Brazil and set you up for two months while you're there."

Suzy's eyes widened, and her mouth fell open. But she remembered her promise to Monica and snapped her jaw shut. Mason was impressed.

"Can you keep your mouth shut, Suzy?" Monica asked.

She nodded and wiped the tears from her face.

"Good. Now go hide in the toilet for ten minutes. Clean yourself up and then get out of here as soon as you can."

Monica released the girl and she made a beeline for the door.

"And Suzy," Monica said, stopping the girl in her tracks. "I'll know if you tell."

The girl's eyes widened, her face drained of color and she turned, hurrying from the room.

"What if she talks?" Mason hissed.

Monica turned to him and her hard eyes made his entire body still. "Like I said. I'll know."

If that was how she'd looked at Suzy, Mason felt they had a chance the girl would keep her mouth shut. But also it didn't matter. Once they got out of here tonight, it wouldn't matter what some scared girl said. No one would find Elijah Moore or Arnold Walsh until The Agency wanted them to be found. *If* they wanted them to be found.

There was a singular, soft knock at the back door.

Mason moved to it and pulled it open. Sanchez was there in tactical gear. Ready. "We've got two," Mason said.

Sanchez nodded and turned to the darkness. Mason moved back into the kitchen. Sanchez and another agent hustled into the house, grabbed Arnold and quickly headed back outside.

"You get back to Kierra and get out of here ASAP," he said to Monica. She nodded and turned to Lane. The look that passed between them was meaningful, although Mason had no idea what it meant. When she was gone, he and Lane grabbed Elijah and headed out of the kitchen. They closed the door behind him and walked off into the night.

A black van was parked a few feet from the kitchen door on a gravel driveway, just outside the arc of light from the house. They hoisted Elijah into the back of the van to the rest of his team and crawled inside behind him. They were moving immediately. Mission accomplished.

seven

"So we'll go to Puerto Rico for two weeks, then back to D.C. so I can take this dumb test and get my raise and then *home*," Kierra called to Monica.

Monica was in the bathroom brushing her hair and Kierra was sitting on their hotel bed, their skin flushed and warm from the shower. Kierra had her tablet on her lap. She was going over their itinerary. She called out to Monica again, "And I just sent my request for paid vacation to you."

"Just sign it, Kierra," Monica yelled back.

Kierra smirked, "Normally I would. But we're technically under high HR alert so you probably shouldn't let me forge your signature anymore." She threw her tablet to the bed as Monica walked out of the bathroom, naked, her inky black hair pulled over one shoulder. "Also," Kierra added with a grin. "That's a violation of the information systems chain of command. I could be stealing money from your accounts hand over fist."

Monica stopped at the end of the bed and reached for Kierra's legs. She pulled her closer and Kierra fell onto her back with a laugh.

"Why steal from us yourself when you can just convince

your best friend to bust our civilian contractors' budget for the final quarter of the year," Monica said, leaning down to untie the knot keeping Kierra's robe closed.

"She was in the middle of a shootout. She earned that money, fair and square," Kierra said, with a hitch of her voice. Monica's hands smoothed up her stomach to cup her breasts.

"Besides, I would hope," Monica said, circling Kierra's nipples with her thumbs, "that if you were going to rob us blind, you'd at least get a new car out of it."

"My car is fine," Kierra said.

Monica crawled over her and sank against her slowly. When they were face to face and breast to breast, Monica's thigh between Kierra's legs, she smiled. "Your car is almost as old as you," she said and kissed her.

Kierra could have buried herself in that kiss. The gentle stroke of their tongues together, the soft pressure of Monica's lips, the scrape of Monica's teeth every now and then. She cupped Monica's face and tried to deepen the kiss, but Monica pulled back. She moved her hand to caress Kierra's bottom lip.

"Are you okay?" Monica whispered.

"I'm fine," Kierra breathed. "This was hardly even a mission at all."

"Maybe. But we can't keep taking you into the field. And technically, when you pass your exam you won't be able to abandon Command to come with us as much as you do."

Kierra frowned. "Well, we're just going to have to find a loophole. You two aren't going to run around the world while I stay home to file your paperwork and bake cookies."

Monica's eyebrows rose. "Can you bake? Can you cook?"

"Of course not. But that's not the point," Kierra said.

"We could hire another personal assistant to replace you," Monica said. She dropped her eyes and watched as her index finger dipped into the adorable indentation on the tip of Kierra's chin.

Kierra pushed Monica off of her onto her back and strad-dled her hips. Monica stared up at her, amusement lighting her eyes. "I let you get away with a lot of shit-"

"You let me?"

"But if you ever mention getting another PA to me again, you won't get a good night's sleep for the rest of your life."

"Are you threatening me?" Monica laughed.

"I sure as fuck am."

"I'm an actual deadly weapon," Monica said, running her hands up Kierra's thighs.

Kierra grabbed Monica's hands and pressed them into the bed over her head. She ground her pussy against Monica's. "Yes you are," Kierra said. She leaned down, hovering her face over Monica's. "And just how long would you last, Ms. Actual Fucking Weapon, if I told you that you couldn't touch or taste me again?"

Monica tilted her head to the side and smiled up at Kierra. "Only me?"

Kierra licked her lips, "Only you. But I would let Lane do *whatever* he wanted with me."

Monica moved her head quickly and Kierra moved away just as fast, dodging her kiss. She released Monica's hands. Monica grabbed her waist and pulled her close, latching her mouth onto Kierra's neck, licking and sucking.

Kierra laughed, moaned and shimmied out of Monica's grasp. She tried to dart up the bed, but Monica turned and grabbed her left ankle, pulling her back, flipping her over. Monica grabbed both of Kierra's ankles and wrapped them around her waist, covering Kierra's body.

"How long would you last?" Kierra asked around a laugh.

"We don't need another PA," Monica said against Kierra's lips before pushing her tongue inside.

"I thought so," Kierra mumbled around their kiss. "Now fuck me, please."

"Don't you want to wait for Lane and Carlisle?"

Kierra wrapped her arms around Monica's neck. "I don't know how to tell you this, but I have *lots* of energy."

"So I've heard," Lane said from the doorway. They turned to him. "Oh, don't mind me. Keep doing what you're doing. Please."

"Please," Kierra whimpered into Monica's ear.

▭

MASON'S TRAINING said that he should get out of Edinburgh as soon as possible. Now that they'd gotten their target and especially because so many people had seen his face at the party, he should be on the move. Now. But he wasn't moving, at least not in the right direction. He was sitting in the back of a cab with Lane, heading to the other man's hotel. He could almost hear Tiya's voice in his head as she'd signed off every episode of Bawdy Boudoir for over a year.

Spend a little time outside of your bubble today, lovers. You deserve it.

HE'D BEEN WONDERING about his bubble for a long while. Ever since the first time he'd laid eyes on Tiya and had to resist the intense urge he felt to go talk to her, because he had been on a mission and couldn't jeopardize his cover. Maybe it was the accumulated influence of Tiya's podcast or his growing desire for her even though he could never fulfill it. Or maybe it was the heady feeling of being just on the margin of Lane, Monica and Kierra. Their bubble seemed much more expansive than his. They jumped wholly into every moment in a way Mason couldn't or wouldn't; he wasn't sure which. They made him wonder if his bubble was only as small as he'd made it. They made him wonder if Tiya was really so far out of his reach.

They made him wonder. And that in and of itself was new and possibly dangerous.

Lane unlocked the hotel room door and walked straight to the bedroom.

Mason could hear soft whispers as Lane pushed the bedroom door open.

"Oh, don't mind me. Keep doing what you're doing. Please."

"Are you alone?" He recognized Monica's voice even though it sounded slightly different; deeper and husky. Full of lust.

Lane stepped further into the room and Mason replaced him in the door frame.

Monica's body was covering Kierra's. Kierra smiled at him. Monica simply took him in. Mason decided not to take that personally, since he'd observed over the course of the day that Monica didn't smile genuinely at anyone besides Kierra.

"Does this mean you've come to play with us?" Kierra asked.

Lane groaned. Mason turned to him and was shocked to see that he was nearly half-undressed. He laughed when they made eye contact. "I don't know how y'all celebrate in black ops. But this works for us." His hands moved to his belt buckle and he raised his eyebrows.

"Yes," Mason croaked.

"Yes what?" Monica demanded. Kierra groaned.

"Yes I-" he turned his gaze back to the bed and swallowed. "Yes, I came to play. Jesus, how do people handle the three of you?"

"You're the first actually," Lane said, his hands gripping him behind the neck and patting his chest. He'd been so entranced by Monica's hard stare that he hadn't even noticed the man walk toward him.

Monica and Kierra crawled up to the head of the bed, Kierra between Monica's spread legs. Kierra smiled as she watched both men undress while Monica ran her hands and her mouth over Kierra's shoulders.

"Condoms?" Mason asked. Kierra moved to the bedside table and pulled out a fresh box.

"We got these just for you," she said, as if it was the most romantic gesture. And it was. Knowing that they had thought about him made something pulse in his chest. How long had it been since someone had thought about him like that? Did Tiya think of him?

Kierra lifted onto her knees and extended a hand to him. "Come here?"

Mason joined them on the bed. Kierra laid him down next to Monica and Lane crawled behind Kierra.

"We won't do anything you don't want," Monica said. "And you can stop anytime."

Mason nodded. They waited in the silent, darkened room. The heat from their bodies comforted him even as he realized that he had no idea what to do next. When had he become this person; so unsure of genuine human interaction?

Eventually, Kierra barged right into the silence, willing to take control; something he guessed was her role in their day-to-day relationship as well. "Can we touch you?" She whispered.

Lane smiled and brushed his mouth against her shoulder.

Mason gulped and nodded, "Yes."

She turned to Lane and grabbed his left hand, resting on her left hip. The question she asked him was silent, and he answered by pressing his mouth to hers as he let her move his hand to Mason's half-hard dick.

Mason hissed and they all turned to him. "Sorry, I just…" He didn't finish the sentence, too ashamed to admit that it had been so long since someone else had touched him that it was a shock.

Kierra smiled kindly down at him. "It's okay," she said as her and Lane's hands stroked him slowly to life. "Does that feel good?"

He nodded.

"Don't mind Kierra," Monica said as she resettled herself onto her side, facing him. "She likes to talk during sex. A lot." Mason saw Lane's other hand reach out and grasp her thigh.

"And don't mind Monica," Kierra said. "She's just mad because I'm directing the show right now."

Monica raised an eyebrow at Mason. She reached out, pulling Kierra down on top of her. "You're so mouthy to me tonight."

Kierra giggled and crawled on top of Monica, "How wet are you about it? Oh no wait, don't tell me. I'll find out for myself."

Mason watched Kierra slither down Monica's body, kissing and licking at her skin before settling between her legs. He moaned as Lane added a wet hand to his dick.

Lane smiled up at him. "Do you want my mouth?" Monica and Kierra both moaned at his words and the way Kierra was rubbing the pads of her fingers along Monica's sex.

"Yes," Mason hissed. His back bowed as Lane squeezed him. He wouldn't last long.

"There's another box of flavored condoms in the drawer if you want. Maya and Kenny approved," Kierra offered helpfully before lowering her mouth to Monica's sex. Monica's back arched from the bed and her eyes closed as she swallowed back her moan. Mason turned to Lane, who was already reaching for the bedside table.

"Maya's got an encyclopedic knowledge of the best-tasting condoms actually," he said and ripped the box open. Soon enough the room filled with the sound of Lane and Kierra's mouths on Mason and Monica's bodies.

If Mason was overcome at Lane and Kierra's hands on

him after so long without touch, he came completely apart when he added his mouth. A strong grip and stroke, lots of tongue and saliva and an insistent suction brought him to orgasm so quickly he was almost embarrassed. But when the lights stopped popping behind his eyelids and the room focused again, he realized that there was no reason to be embarrassed. Lane's smile was filthy, and his erection was standing at attention as he raised onto his knees. He patted Mason on his stomach. Mason jumped; his body was so sensitive.

"Rest up," he said, as he moved behind Kierra and slipped his dick inside of her. She moaned.

Monica was pinching her nipples hard and she laughed, "Not so mouthy now, are you?"

Mason stroked himself slowly as Kierra lowered her mouth; a wicked gleam in her eyes. Monica hissed. Mason had to lift onto his side to see Kierra's fingers sawing into Monica, punishing her as she glared up her body. And Monica glared back.

Their exchange made Mason want to laugh. Lane shrugged at him as he moved slowly in and out of Kierra. Apparently, this was a normal occurrence for them. Mason felt overcome by the warmth of their sex. The gentle way they touched each other exactly as the other person liked. Kierra's fingers and mouth on Monica, making the normally stoic and silent woman come apart, moans falling from her lips, her cries getting louder and louder. And Lane's deep strokes, his fingers digging into Kierra's waist as the two of them tried to stave off their own orgasms to draw out the moment. Waiting, Mason finally realized, until Monica arched up, pulling Kierra's face to hers and kissing her deeply as she came on her fingers.

Mason was hard again, stroking himself faster as Kierra called out her own orgasm into Monica's mouth and Lane followed them all, shouting out his release as Monica stroked his cheek lovingly.

"Fuck," Mason ground out, falling onto his back, shocked as his dick emptied over his stomach and hand. "Oh fuck," he breathed, chest heaving. "I haven't come twice in one night in so long."

Lane laughed. "Happy we could help," he said as he collapsed onto the bed.

"How long since you've come three times?" Kierra asked, smiling down at him.

Mason's mouth fell open.

"Let him come down, sweet girl," Monica whispered to Kierra, turning her face to capture her lips.

EVERY WEEK TIYA solicited stories under the theme "new experiences" and her listeners sent in stories, some real, some fiction. Mason usually avoided this theme because it had been so long since he'd had any new experiences that didn't involve bulletproof vests or end in the screech of wheels on a high-stakes extraction.

But this was absolutely a new experience.

He was bent over the foot of the bed, one of Lane's hands rubbing his back and shoulders, soothing him, as the other guided his latex-covered dick into his ass, slowly and with lots of lube. But he'd sent a story like this in once about a study trip abroad to Greece from college – back when life was simpler and normal. So that part wasn't entirely new.

The new experience was watching Kierra lower herself onto Monica's strap-on, a dirty smile on her face and her eyes on Mason. She waited for Lane to begin moving in and out of him to start moving herself. Mason watched as she tried to match Lane's pace and it was too much. Monica's hands snaked around Kierra's body to massage her breasts, pinching and rolling her nipples as she lazily watched Mason and Lane over Kierra's shoulder.

"How does he feel?" Monica asked.

Lane's only reply was a wild grunt as his hips moved faster. Monica moved one of her hands down Kierra's stomach to the crest of her thighs. Kierra's head fell back as she came with a shout. Her hips never stopped moving.

Mason wanted to taste her, and he moved unexpectedly away from Lane, crawling up the bed until he was in front of her.

Lane laughed and the bed shifted as he followed.

He locked eyes with Monica, "May I?"

She licked up Kierra's neck and whispered into her ear.

"Yes, oh god, fuck yes," Kierra screamed.

Mason moved his mouth to Kierra's free nipple and sucked it into his mouth as Lane entered him again slowly. He moaned around Kierra's breast and her own cries became keening wails.

"Touch yourself," Monica commanded.

Mason didn't have to look at her to know that she was talking to him. And he was grateful to her as his own hand closed around his leaking erection.

Lane fell over his back and whispered into his ear, "She likes a bit of teeth sometimes." So he scraped his teeth along Kierra's nipples. She shuddered and moaned.

She lifted her head and grabbed at his face, pulling it from her breast. She kissed him, deep and desperate and hungry, as Lane and Monica continued to fuck them into oblivion. The kiss devolved into moans and cries and tongues and teeth until they were holding one another's sweat-slicked bodies, panting and shivering and begging for more.

The sounds of orgasms rising around him and his own approaching release should have been the focal point of his entire world. But it wasn't.

Just as his balls pulled close to his body, he thought of her, her voice invading his brain.

"Think of me, lovers."

He did think of Tiya Randall. He imagined her in her studio, in headphones recording her podcast. He imagined her hunched on a bus heading to work, her face buried in a book. And he conjured his favorite surveillance image of her walking down the street with her best friend, laughing, just as he shot one more load all over the bed. Of course he thought of Tiya. And that was the problem.

KIERRA DIDN'T FALL ASLEEP SO MUCH as pass out from the best kind of exhaustion. That easy gray moment after she had finally expended all of the adrenaline running through her veins after time in the field was the best part of her day. She slept deeply and peacefully; dead to the world for hours after. But not tonight.

Tonight Kierra woke with a start to faint popping sounds in the distance. She bolted straight up in bed, her chest heaving and her eyes slowly adjusting to the dark room. She looked around the bed. Monica was asleep on one side of her and Lane on the other. She frowned. Apparently, Carlisle had left like a thief in the night. She heard the popping again and crawled out of bed. She was shocked when she pulled the curtain aside and saw fireworks. She'd completely forgotten that it was New Year's Eve. Well, New Year's Day now.

"It's just fireworks," Lane mumbled from the bed.

"I know," she said. "I can't believe it's a new year though."

Lane pushed the sheet off his body. He walked across the room toward her. "Is that a bad thing?" He asked, wrapping his warm, naked body around hers. They stared out at the fireworks.

It was one of the least sexual hugs he'd ever given her. It reminded her of why she'd quickly become so infatuated with him and why she assumed Monica had fallen for him as well. Lane was warm and open and never missed a moment to reassure the people around him that they were not alone. She leaned into his embrace.

"It's not a bad thing. I just can't believe how quickly this year passed. How much has changed."

She didn't need to explain the changes she meant.

"What did you do last New Year's Eve?" He whispered into her hair.

She smiled, "Maya and I bought tickets to a party at this club. We bought new dresses and shoes. Our makeup was immaculate."

"Did you have fun?" Monica asked groggily from the bed.

Kierra turned toward her. All she could see was her silhouette, her head propped on her arm. "No," Kierra laughed. "The line to get in was so long that Maya put her flats on before we even got to the door. The drinks were overpriced and watered down. And the stench of cologne was so thick I got a headache. We were home in our pajamas on the couch with wine way before the ball dropped."

Lane squeezed her to him.

"What did you two do?" She felt Lane's chuckle before she heard it.

"Oh, nothing much," he whispered.

"We were in Nicaragua tracking down a CEO who'd raided his employees' pensions and fled a conviction for insider trading," Monica added.

"That sounds more exciting than my night," Kierra said.

"It was," Lane replied. "But we missed you."

"We'd have rather been on that couch with you," Monica said.

Kierra didn't want to cry. It seemed so ridiculous to do that. But her eyes filled with tears before she could stop it. She nodded absently, a loud explosion of sparklers catching her eye. She turned back to the window and smiled through her happy tears.

"Next time," she said, pulling Lane's arms tighter around her. "Next year we'll be very low-key and boring. Together."

Tiya Randall opened her eyes and enjoyed the soft fuzzy look of her bedroom first thing in the morning. She always loved the gray of not-quite sunrise. Everything felt dreamlike and her poor eyesight only added to the illusion. She put off cramming her glasses onto her face until she absolutely had to get out of bed. Those blurry moments of almost awake were usually the best of her day. Before she had to check her email, trudge into work and pretend as if her boss's barking orders at the staff was perfectly normal. Before she had to hide in an empty cubicle at the back of the office to eat her lunch in peace. Before she had to wade through the early evening rush on public transportation, avoiding the lecherous men staring at her, the teenagers looking for any opportunity to assert their dominance over… the world, and old ladies with grocery carts. And before she had to scarf down her dinner before her second favorite part of the day. The moment when she could shut the door on her small second bedroom and record the latest segment of her weekly podcast, Bawdy Boudoir.

She would have complained about her landlord calling it a second bedroom except a carefully worded verbal threat about reporting her to the Housing Authority had gotten Tiya a rent reduction that made the apartment just inside her budget. She'd had to give up the idea of having a roommate, but she'd quickly recognized that her spare room could be the perfect space for recording her podcast. The podcast that all of her friends dismissed as a strange hobby and technically cost her more money than it made but was her actual dream job.

The email notification on her phone chimed. She groaned and turned over in bed. It was her mother. She just knew it. She could feel it in her bones. Her mother loved to send emails to her only daughter first thing in the morning with a roundup of her favorite online conspiracy theories about aliens, new deals on subscriptions to online dating apps and a rundown of her latest dream premonitions of when and where Tiya would meet her future husband. Her mother was well-meaning and undeterred; just because none of her dreams had ever come true didn't mean that one wouldn't.

Tiya closed her eyes and prayed for patience as she groped on the other side of the bed for her cell phone. She pulled it toward her, forgetting that it was plugged into the charger on the wall. She raised the phone and the charging cord above her face and squinted with her stronger eye, trying to read the email.

The email wasn't from her mother.

Tiya dropped the phone onto her bed and sat up excitedly. She snatched her glasses from her nightstand and shoved them onto her face. She turned on the bedside lamp and laid back down, grabbing her phone again.

The email was from him.

Tiya had just started Bawdy Boudoir when she got the first email from Jarhead. At the time, her listeners were still in the single digits and she knew all of them in real life. So finding out that someone who didn't know her personally – or remember what she'd looked like with braces – was listening had made her ecstatic. The letter had made her wet. Just like every letter he'd sent her. Her thighs clenched in anticipation.

Dear Love-
I've been thinking about you. I know I write that every time. I mean it every time. But this email is different. Normally, when I think of you, I'm alone. Naked. Sometimes wet. Always hard.

TIYA MOANED and slipped her hand under her covers into her underwear.

Do you think about me? Are you wet?

SHE WAS.

But this time when I thought about you, I wasn't alone.

TIYA SWALLOWED the irrational feeling of jealousy. She didn't even know what he looked like, his real name or how he liked his coffee. She didn't have a right to be jealous. And yet she was.

You might not believe this, but I've never had a very active sex life. A few girlfriends.
A date every now and then. A quick hookup in a bar. Always me and someone else.

TIYA INHALED SHARPLY, guessing where this could go. Her fingers circled her clit lazily.

But like I said, this time was different. I was at a work engagement when I met a man.
Nice eyes. Great smile. Thick dick.

"HOLY SHIT," Tiya breathed as she slipped two fingers into her clenching sex.

Anyway, this man and I were working on a project together. It was all very boring office stuff. But when it was over…

TIYA MOANED AGAIN. He always had the best ellipses.

He and I met up with some other colleagues for a celebratory drink that turned into more. This time it wasn't just me and someone else. It was me… and him… and her… and… her.

"OH MY GOD," Tiya groaned as she pumped her fingers into her pussy faster. Her legs fell open.

It was the best night of my life in some ways. All that skin and wet flesh and teeth and tongues and those moans and cries and brief, delicious flashes of pain as he fucked me.

TIYA THOUGHT she should slow down. She was so close and didn't want to come before the story was over. But she couldn't stop herself. Couldn't stop imagining his words. Couldn't stop imagining the face she always gave him and conjuring the scene he painted in her head. Wishing that she'd been there. Always wishing that this were real.

It was amazing. But all I could think about was you. What if you were there? How would you taste on my tongue? How would you feel around my dick? What would my name sound like on your lips?

TIYA DROPPED her phone and came in a wet gush around her fingers, her jaw clenched, her hips locking, her back arching and her free hand clutching her bedsheets. She closed her eyes and panted through her orgasm as the soft gray of the almost sunrise became the yellowy light of morning. When her breathing had slowed, she grabbed her phone again.

Maybe one day we'll meet. Maybe one day I'll know the answer to these questions and a million others. Or maybe this is all we'll ever have. It's worth it to have even just this with you.
P.S.
This story was for us, not the podcast. I hope you have a great day. Think of me when you touch yourself.

"EVERY TIME, LOVER," she whispered to her empty room. "Every time." Eventually Tiya pulled her hand from her underwear, crawled out of bed and padded to the shower to start her day. A bright smile on her face. If only every day started so well.

His Only Valentine

89

Content Warnings

Fist fight
Shooting death

———————

one

———————

"Maya," Kenny called out as he unlocked Maya's front door and let himself into her apartment. "Maya!"

"Oh my god, stop yelling. I'm in the kitchen," she yelled back.

He tossed her spare key into the bowl she kept on a low table by the front door and smiled. She hated when he yelled. He closed and locked her front door behind him, kicked off his shoes, pulled his messenger bag over his head and dropped it onto one of her dining room chairs.

He found her leaning over a counter, scrolling on her cell phone with one hand and holding an orange slice in the other. Her new honey blonde braids were piled on top of her head in a messy bun that he found ridiculously endearing. He stepped into the kitchen and closed his mouth over the piece of fruit, licking her fingers. She didn't stop scrolling on her phone but moved her other hand to the plate in front of her, grabbed another slice and held it out to him. He smiled and ate that one as well, sucking at her fingers again. He moved into the kitchen and settled behind her, covering her body with his own.

"What are you doing here?" she asked, her eyes still on her phone.

He looked briefly at her screen and recognized the ChatBot stats page. He bit her shoulder lightly. "We're filming tonight," he said.

"Not for a few hours." She put her phone down and stood up straight, turning around to face him.

He stepped back and greedily drank her in with his eyes as his mouth went dry. Maya never wore many clothes around her apartment, especially now that Kierra had moved out and she was curiously procrastinating about choosing another roommate. Kenny wasn't in a hurry for her to get a new roommate; not just because he liked having her all to himself but also because he loved having her all to himself while she was nearly naked. She wore a tight, long-sleeved gray shirt, just long enough to skim her hips, stopping at the top of a very brief pair of panties.

His entire focus got lost in the crease of her thighs.

She cleared her throat and he smiled, letting his gaze ascend her body slowly. He got a little lost again taking in the small raised fabric where her nipples were hidden, and he wondered if they were hardening for him or if that was just his imagination. When he finally lifted his head to look at her face, there was a small grin on her mouth and mirth in her eyes. He felt certain that he would never get over how beautiful she was.

"I thought you'd want to go home and shower or nap before you came over here," she said.

He shook his head. "I can do all of those things here. With you."

Her grin turned to a smile as a soft blush appeared on the tops of her cheeks. He leaned down and kissed her softly; a gentle, teasing brush of their lips. She ran her hands up his chest and wrapped them around his neck, pulling his body against hers.

"Did you miss me today?" she whispered against his lips.

"Of course. Did you miss me?"

"A whole lot," she said, before slipping her tongue into his mouth.

He ran his hands down her back, over her hips and caressed the globes of her ass. She giggled when he dug his fingers into the soft flesh, pulling her closer as he moved his hands down the backs of her thighs, loving the way the soft dimpled flesh felt against the pads of his fingers, against his shoulders, on top of his thighs. In fact, every bit of her skin felt perfect against his.

She nibbled at his bottom lip, which made all of the blood in his body rush south. He groaned into her mouth, grabbed her thighs and lifted her against him.

"Oh my god, Kenny," she gasped around a giggle. "You have to stop picking me up."

He nipped at her chin. "Why?"

"I'm not small," she said.

His fingers dug into her flesh and he smiled against her mouth. "Believe me, I know," he whispered reverently as he set her onto the counter.

She wrapped her legs around his waist and pulled him close.

"I can bench press more than you weigh," he said as he smoothed his palms up and down her thighs.

She lifted one eyebrow, "And what if I gain weight?"

He smiled, "You might not know this since you hate weights-"

"Very much. They're evil."

He laughed and continued as if she hadn't interrupted him. "I can literally just add more weight to the machine. Gain all the weight you want."

She moved her hands to his face and ran her thumbs over his cheeks, "And you're just going to keep picking me up?"

"As long as you'll let me," he whispered.

She leaned over and gave him a peck on the lips. "Good." And then she went in for a real kiss.

He kissed her back, nice and slow, feeding her his tongue to rub along hers; the exact way he'd been dreaming of kissing her all day as he tried to catch up on his paperwork and coordinate a surveillance operation in Mexico City on a suspect in an international money laundering case. All with a glaring Kierra watching his every move.

When Kenny pulled back from their kiss, Maya placed small pecks down his chin and along his jaw, still looking for an as-yet-undiscovered ticklish spot on his body. She laughed more than he did in her search, but his entire body felt as if it was buzzing with electricity at her touch so he happily tilted his head back, giving her full access to him.

"Any idea what you want to do tonight?" he asked as she licked his Adam's apple.

She leaned back and looked at him with a dirty smile. "I ran a poll for my viewers," she said. "And doggy style won out. You okay with that?"

He chuckled, "I'm not even going to dignify that with an answer." He squeezed her thighs. "Do we have time to fool around beforehand?"

She sucked her bottom lip into her mouth and fluttered her eyelashes at him. He swallowed and waited. She flattened her hands on his chest and slid them south as she answered. "That's up to you, babe. Will you be able to get hard for the show tonight?"

His hands moved up her legs over her stomach. Her mouth fell open on a soft gasp as he rubbed her nipples through her shirt. "When have I ever not been able to get hard for you?"

She smiled wickedly at him and ran her hands over the front of his pants, unzipping his slacks with shaky hands. He kept his eyes on her as his hands plucked at her nipples.

"Wait," he said quickly, pulling back from the counter.

She frowned at him.

Kenny leaned over to kiss her frown quickly and then he pulled his cell phone and wallet from his back pockets.

She squinted her eyes at him and folded her arms across her chest.

He tossed his phone on the counter and opened his wallet. "You want ribbed or regular?"

"What?"

"Ribbed or regular?" he repeated.

Her eyebrows lifted. "You have a selection of condoms in your wallet?"

He put his wallet next to his phone and lifted an eyebrow at her. He held the condoms up with one hand and smiled. "Not just any condom selection."

She laughed as she saw that he was holding three condoms: one regular, one ribbed and one flavored. All from her favorite brand. She plucked the ribbed condom from his fingers and smiled. "You're a really fucking great boyfriend, babe," she said sweetly and then ripped the foil wrapper open.

His heart began to beat faster. He pushed his briefs over his hips and stroked his already hard dick.

She impatiently pushed his hand out of the way and squeezed the head, pulling a groan from his throat. He was panting as she rolled the condom down his penis. "You want to practice for tonight?" she asked breathlessly.

He shook his head sharply. "I'm pretty sure we can get the hang of it." And then he grabbed her face, "This time I want to watch you while you come. I haven't seen you since this morning."

She giggled and he tasted her happiness with his tongue. "Anything for you," she whispered into his mouth. He shivered.

He helped her scoot to the edge of the counter and lifted her left leg onto his shoulder. He kissed her ankle and squeezed himself as she pulled the gusset of her panties aside.

He ran the tip of his dick along her wet cleft. They both groaned. "Put me inside you, baby," he whispered.

"God, you're demanding after work. I like it." She held him and angled the head at her opening. Their eyes locked as he slid into her slowly. They both pressed their lips shut trying to stop the smiles that wanted to spread across their mouths, muffling the moans building in their throats. They held their breath as their bodies joined painfully slow. When he was inside her to the hilt, they both stilled, panting, staring at one another, her pussy pulsing around his dick. They'd missed each other.

"So Valentine's Day is in a few days," she gasped as he pulled out of her just as slowly as he'd entered.

"It is."

"Got any plans?" she asked quickly before her head dropped back and a breathy moan fell from her lips. He sank back into her wet heat.

"I have lots of plans," he said, each word a panting moan.

"You wanna share?" she moaned back.

"It's a surprise, Maya," his voice desperate as he pushed her shirt over her breasts.

She helped him and then clenched around his dick when he started rolling her nipples between his fingers.

His back bowed and he shuddered. "Shit." He started to move in and out of her, faster and faster, in long strokes that he knew touched all her favorite spots.

"Oh fuck," she groaned. "I hate surprises. Oh fuck, right there."

He took one hand from her breasts, licked his thumb and moved his hand between their bodies to rub small circles over her clit.

She cried out and she replaced his hand with her own, raising her nipple to her mouth. He growled and momentarily lost his rhythm. She laughed and then her long tongue snaked out to lick the swell of her breast.

They both moaned. His hips moved faster.

"Let me surprise you, Maya. I just want to give you everything you deserve," he said, playing with her clit as a distraction.

She'd spent the last two weeks trying to get him to tell her what he'd planned for their first Valentine's Day together. She'd even deputized Kierra to surveil him while they were at work, which is why she'd spent the entire day glaring at him and finding any reason to peek at his computer screen. It was adorable although Kierra could be kind of terrifying when she wanted. But he'd managed to keep his secret, even though it went against his base instinct to give Maya everything she wanted and to never lie to her again.

But he wasn't sure how long he would be able to keep his mouth shut. Maya was not at all above using her body to get what she wanted from him and he was oh so willing to be seduced. It should have been a short-lived cat and mouse game. Every time they'd touched, he'd been imbued with an all-consuming fear that he would spill the details about their day as he filled a condom or in the drowsy, post-orgasmic haze with her body wrapped in his arms. The only reason he'd managed to keep his plans to himself was that he wanted to surprise her more than anything and she was technically going to be his first Valentine ever. This was a momentous occasion, even if she didn't know it.

So he pumped his hips into her harder and circled her clit and bit his lips closed, focusing on temporarily fucking away her curiosity. She dropped her hands to the counter and he grabbed onto her hips, fucking her with everything he had, holding onto this secret for all he was worth. He'd need to take a shower and a nap before they filmed tonight. But he'd be alright. And most importantly, his plans for their first Valentine's Day together – the first of what he knew would be many – would still be a secret for one more day.

––––––––––––––––––

two

––––––––––––––––––

Maya woke up slowly, the way she'd been waking up more mornings than not for months: in Kenny's arms. And just like every other morning she'd drifted to consciousness enveloped by him, she turned to bury her face into her pillow, hiding her smile from the dark room. And like every other morning, he unconsciously tightened his arms around her when she moved, which only made her smile widen against her pillow. The bright, shiny newness of their relationship hadn't even begun to wear off and every day Maya wondered if it ever would. 'Could it get any better than this?' she'd think to herself. And then he would bury his face in the crook of her neck in his sleep and she'd turn to brush her mouth across his forehead. Every morning, this sequence of events would let her know, from some deep-seated place in her stomach, that it could get better than this. And it would. And then she'd have to bury her smile in her pillow again.

But there really wasn't a template to her mornings with Kenny, especially not once he woke up. Sometimes he had enough time to hang around and fuck her slowly, slipping out of bed as she drifted back to sleep. Some mornings he was already dressed when she woke up and he put a soft kiss on her cheek on his way out. And sometimes they didn't even make it to the morning. She'd get out of bed in the middle of the night to go to the bathroom and instead of Kenny's hard body next to her, she'd find a small post-it note with a careful apology scribbled on it. So when Maya was lucky enough to wake up in Kenny's arms, she usually liked to relish it.

But today was different. Today, as soon as she managed to shrink her smile a bit, she started to fidget because it was time to get to work. Maya didn't like surprises. She liked order and respected plans. Even more than that, she respected plans that she made. So the fact that Kenny was keeping the details for their first Valentine's Day together a secret was unacceptable. How was she supposed to plan an outfit for this?! Okay and also, she admitted, running her nails over his scalp, she was nervous. This was their *first* Valentine's Day together. She needed to know what they would be doing so she could temper her excitement. She wanted so much for this day to be perfect, but she knew it couldn't be.

Maya hadn't been in many full-blown relationships in her life but the most consistent thing about Valentine's with all of her exes had been a deep pit of terrible. In high school, she'd let her first real boyfriend take her out to a dinner date during their sophomore year and then been forced to empty her purse to pay for dinner when he realized he didn't have enough money to cover their meals. She'd never been more pissed in her young life. The fancy dinner had been his idea. She'd just wanted to go to the movies. She had dumped him on the sidewalk outside of the restaurant and taken the bus home. Her first girlfriend in college had spun a long yarn about not believing in the capitalism of Valentine's Day. She'd declined to make plans with Maya so she could "meditate." When Maya ran into her at the movies with the girl who was supposed to be just her roommate, she'd dumped almost fifteen dollars' worth of snacks onto her head. It was the best money Maya had spent that night, since the movie she and

Kierra saw had sucked. Ever since then, Maya had usually spent every February 14th with Kierra, eating ice cream and drinking cocktails and watching the best – or worst – action movies they could find. But this year Kierra was going to be with her bosses, probably dressing up in black-tie attire and fucking each other in the middle of Times Square or whatever it was those three got up to. And she would be with Kenny.

Kenny had been hinting for weeks that he'd planned the perfect day for them. Maya was charmed and dismayed because she believed him. For the first time since she was a teenager, she found herself really looking forward to Valentine's Day. Trusting him was a new and terrifying place to be. If only she could get him to give up an itemized itinerary with weather information, then maybe she could relax. Maybe.

"Stop rocking," Kenny mumbled into her shoulder.

"Make me," she said and arched her back to press her ass into his groin.

He moved one hand to her hip and gripped her there hard. She sucked in a breath and held it in anticipation. But then he scraped his teeth along the skin at her neck. "Not now. I have to head into Command." She frowned as he crawled out of bed.

She turned and looked up at him. "Why? Stay here with me." The "naked in bed" was silent and very much implied.

He shook his head, "I can't. I need to make sure that all of my cases are squared away before-"

She sat up quickly. "Before what? Before we go on a trip? Are we going out of town? Some place cold? Hot? International?" She peppered him with questions but he turned and literally ran to the bathroom. "Just tell me already!" Maya called after him. He didn't respond.

⬜

"THREE MORE DAYS," Kenny mumbled to himself as he stepped into Maya's shower. He only had to keep this secret for three more days and about ten hours. All he had to do was shower, get dressed and escape Maya's apartment before she fully woke up and he'd have nine hours where his secret was relatively safe. Relatively, because the closer they got to the day, the harder Maya pressed him and the more he wanted to give in.

Maybe under other circumstances – maybe if he had another job – he wouldn't feel the need to hold onto the details so tightly. But Kenny was keenly aware that they'd only have so many firsts and he wanted them to savor each and every one of them. He wanted to surprise her. He wanted their first Valentine's Day together to be perfect. And to do that, all he had to do was keep his mouth closed for a little while longer, he reminded himself over and over again as he washed his body. But his shoulders tensed when he heard the bathroom door creak open. He tried to prepare himself to survive – and also thoroughly enjoy – her next gambit as his dick hardened in anticipation. She pulled the shower curtain back and he turned toward her. She was leaning inside, her bottom lip in her mouth as she stared at his ass.

"Is there room in there for two?" she asked innocently.

He turned fully around and her eyes settled on his hardening dick. She licked her lips, then she moved back and the shower curtain fell closed. He stepped out of the water's spray and opened the curtain again. He couldn't help but smile as she pulled her tank top over her head. She winked at him as she dropped it to the floor and grabbed the thin side straps of her underwear. He started to stroke himself slowly behind the curtain as she bent over to push her underwear down her legs and she stepped out of them. He swallowed a groan at the gentle sway of her heavy breasts.

She smiled wickedly as she walked toward the shower, her beautiful body bouncing with every step. He wondered if her heart was beating faster like his was as the anticipation built. He wondered if this would be the time when she won and he broke down and told her everything. And then he wondered if her blood ran cold as the sound of his text message alert cut through the lust in the bathroom's damp air and the din of running shower. He growled in his throat and stepped out of the shower. Maya laughed.

He grabbed his phone from the counter and frowned down at the screen and the urgent message there. "I have to go in early," he said.

She looked at him over her left shoulder, her body half inside the shower stall. "Pity. I'll think of you when I'm getting myself off."

He walked to her and brushed a kiss against her cheek. "You better," he whispered against her skin.

▭

HALF AN HOUR LATER, Kenny was rushing through the kitchen at Lane, Monica and Kierra's house. He didn't know what would make Monica call him in early, but he was thankful that she'd saved him from yet another chance for Maya to pull his Valentine's plans from him with her hands or mouth or breasts or cunt. Or hell, her laugh. He was an absolute sucker for her laugh.

He pushed through the secret door in the pantry and headed down into Command, turning right toward the briefing room. Monica and Lane were standing at the head of the table, talking quietly to each other when he came in. Kenny stopped short, "I'm sorry. Are you busy?"

"No, no. Come in," Monica called. "Thank you for getting here so quickly."

"Absolutely," Kenny said.

Lane stood off to the side and Monica crossed her arms over her chest. "I'm really sorry to have to do this to you."

Kenny's steps faltered and his eyebrows bunched together. "Do what?"

"I'm going to have to cancel your day off on Valentine's Day."

"No," Kenny hissed. "No, I still have so much time off left to use. You signed off on it."

"Sorry to break this to you, kid, but all time off is contingent on The Agency's needs," Lane said. "This isn't the kind of job we can sleep on. Besides, you should take this as a compliment. The Agency *needs you*. Congratulations!" Lane's voice was nonchalant, easy, as if every word wasn't shredding weeks of plans. Actually Lane was ruining almost a year of planning and dreaming, but Kenny didn't like to count the time before he and Maya were officially dating. It sounded creepy. Still, the point was that he had been meticulously planning his first Valentine's Day with Maya for so long, in his dreams and in reality, and it was all going up in smoke in seconds.

"Please," Kenny whispered. "Please don't do this to me."

Kenny wasn't sure that it was possible for Lane to be contrite, but his voice seemed a good facsimile. "Sorry, Kenny, we don't have a choice," he breathed with a soft shake of his head.

Monica turned to the smart screen and tapped it on.

Kenny sighed as soon as he saw the man on the screen and he fell into the nearest chair.

"This is the Crown Prince Mohammed of Qatar. He's next in line for the throne. His father has been trusting him with more and more state functions over the past few years, leading to speculation that he might abdicate early and mentor his son on the throne to ease the transition."

"I know," Kenny breathed wearily. "I've been processing press and covert coverage of the Prince for a few months."

"Then you also know that he's in Hong Kong right now to convene the Oil Exporters Summit."

Kenny nodded as his head fell into his hands.

Monica continued briefing him. "Yesterday, an agent intercepted some intel that suggests there might be an assassination attempt on the Prince during his summit."

"Intel from who?" Kenny asked without lifting his head.

"A Swedish asset heard it secondhand from a Chinese businessman with Russian contacts."

Kenny raised his head and squinted his eyes at Monica. "You're canceling my time off for that? That's hardly credible. Can't you send literally anyone else to run interference?"

"We honestly don't know if it's credible," Lane agreed.

"Okay so send Asif or someone else."

"We thought of sending Asif, but we've contracted Chanté to help with remote surveillance and she's refusing to work support for him."

Kenny's jaw ticked and he made a mental note to add this to the list of reasons why he couldn't stand Asif. It was a very long list. "Look," he started, desperate to change their mind. "Everything I know about the royal family's security personnel indicates that they're incredibly loyal and paid well to ensure that that doesn't change. They'll protect the Prince with their lives. Why don't we just pass the information on to them?"

Monica frowned, because of course she'd considered that. "The intel left open the possibility that it could be an inside job."

Kenny could feel his last shred of hope slipping away. "Why can't you two go?" he asked, suddenly so weary.

Monica uncrossed her arms and put her hands onto her hips. Something about the move made Kenny sit up straight and give her his full attention. "Your areas of expertise are covert surveillance and security, yes?" she asked.

"Yes."

"You speak Arabic, yes?"

He wanted to lie but couldn't. "Yes."

"And did you not, in your transfer application, indicate that you would like to achieve the rank of senior agent?"

That had seemed like the most diplomatic way of saying that he wanted to follow in Monica's footsteps. But she probably knew that, just like she knew the answer to this question. To all of these questions. "Yes," he ground out.

"Then this is the mission for you. Consider it a trial run," she said with a small smile. "We can move forward with your training once you're back."

"I had plans," he whispered pathetically, slumping forward again.

"Yes," Monica said. "Kierra told us. We are sorry. But Prince Mohammed's safety is more important than your date."

"No, it's not," Kenny said automatically. The part of his brain that wanted to be Monica in a few years, that knew you were never supposed to tell your superior agent that something mattered more than the mission, that hated the idea of letting anyone know how important Maya was to him knew that this was the worst thing he could have said. But the part of his heart that wanted Maya – only Maya – wouldn't let him take those words back.

"I agree," Monica said. Kenny wasn't sure, but he thought he heard a smile in her voice. "We all have to make sacrifices for the work."

Monica's eyes shifted to the hallway. He heard Kierra's heels striking the floor. He turned as she poked her head into the room. "Did you tell him?" she whispered.

"Yep," Lane said.

She frowned as she walked toward him. "I'm sorry, Ken Doll."

He was too sad to cringe at his nickname. "How do I tell her?" he breathed.

"Tell who what?" she asked as she hopped onto the table next to him and put a comforting hand on his shoulder.

He rolled his eyes. "Tell Maya that I have to cancel our Valentine's plans."

Kierra sighed. The sigh was weary, annoyed and full of pity. "I don't know what they do to you all in The Academy but honestly, it's so sad."

"Kierra," he said. Maybe pleaded?

"Maya knows your life is unpredictable. Tell her you need to run a job and then take her with you. Duh! That's what these two do with me."

"You're our assistant," Lane corrected.

She nodded and then winked at Kenny. "Yeah. That's why."

Kenny shook his head. "I can't. Not again."

"Well, technically you can," she said and turned to Monica, who switched the smart screen to another page. "The Summit is being held at the luxury Royal Garden Palace hotel. I booked the lower penthouse suite." She cringed at Kenny almost apologetically, "The Prince has the upper floors. The hotel has literally all of the amenities. Your suite has a great shower and I'm having Chanté hack into their luxury spa's appointment management system to get our girl a full day of relaxing treatments.

If you're careful, you can intercept the assassination attempt against the Prince *and* give my best friend the best Valentine's Day of her life." She leaned forward and whispered, "But if we're being honest, the best V-day of her life so far was that time in college when she was a featured performer in the Vagina Monologues and her trifling ex-girlfriend showed up late, but with flowers. Truly, the bar is the floor. This might not be as sentimental as your original plans, which were…?"

Kenny rolled his eyes, "I'm not telling you."

"Well anyway, I have faith in your gift-buying skills. You'll be great."

"No," Kenny hissed again. "I can't."

"You can't? Or you won't?" she asked. "Take her or don't, that's totally up to you. But if you make my girl cry, I'll stab you."

He scrubbed his face and turned to Monica.

Monica nodded. "You have permission to bring her. We all have to make sacrifices, but we don't have to deprive ourselves of happiness," she said as she walked from the head of the room. "But we're not authorized to pay even one dollar of hazard pay to her. The auditor made a vague threat against our lives if she saw Maya's bank account number in her system again. So be careful with her." She squeezed his shoulder as she passed and then helped Kierra from the table. Kenny watched as they walked from the room holding hands. Kierra turned toward Lane and winked.

The other man chuckled and began to walk toward the door. He turned to Kenny and smiled. "We're letting you use the jet as a consolation. There'll be tactical support on the ground. You need to be at the airfield in three hours. Good luck," he said quickly, following his wife and girlfriend from the room. Leaving Kenny alone to figure out what to do.

<hr>

MAYA WAS IN HER BEDROOM, poring over her Valentine's lingerie choices, matching her jewelry to each lacy piece and jotting down some notes for possible makeup looks. She also wanted to coordinate her presents to each outfit, but she just couldn't decide. She'd never felt so nervous about seducing a man before.

She grabbed the black frilly lace top and held it up to her body with one hand. She turned to her floor-length mirror. "Hair up? Hair down?" she whispered to herself, her braids held at the crown of her head with her other hand. "Lip gloss? Lipstick?" She let her hair go and shook her head, still unsure. She turned back to the bed, moving the smaller wrapped box next to the cream piece of lingerie and the slightly bigger box next to the black one. She chewed her bottom lip and stared down at her current configuration.

She heard the front door open and her eyes widened. She snatched everything on her bed and stuffed it all into the bag on the floor. She hurriedly shoved the bag back into her closet, just behind her laundry basket and shut the door quietly.

"Maya," Kenny called.

"Coming," she called back, checking her reflection in her mirror. She pulled the lapels of her robe open just a bit more to distract him from noticing that she definitely looked like she had a secret.

"Hey," she said when she walked into the living room. "You're back early. Is everything okay?"

He was pacing the length of her living room. So everything was not okay, she surmised.

He stopped and shook his head at her. "I have to…" He swallowed and shook his head again. "I have a mission. I need to fly to Hong Kong in a few hours."

"Okay," she said with a shrug, relaxing. "I know you have to travel for work. You didn't have to come all the way back here to tell me." She smiled, "That was really sweet though."

He shook his head again, "That's not it. I'm… I'm going to have to cancel our Valentine's Day plans."

It was Maya's turn to shake her head. "Why? It's two days away."

His eyebrows bunched together. "I know but I can't get there, complete the mission and get back in time. I just can't."

"Oh." Maya felt foolish. She clutched the lapels of her robe closed, covering her chest and tried to stop the tears forming in her eyes. It was just a made-up holiday, she thought to herself, calling on all of the defenses she'd created after years alone. It didn't matter. She dropped her gaze to the floor, smiled and shook her head. "That's okay. I understand. I'll be okay on my own. It's actually a really lucrative day to be a cam model," she said with a hollow laugh. It was technically true. Maya could rake in a lot of money in the days just before and just after Valentine's Day, catering to all the sad, lonely single people on the internet. She could pad her rent fund for the next few months on private shows alone. She should have been happy about that, but she wasn't.

She hadn't needed to think twice when Kenny asked her to take Valentine's Day off this year. She'd been more than happy to clear her schedule to spend the day with him. It was a no-brainer that a day basking in his presence was more valuable than the extra bump in her ledger. More valuable even than maybe getting on the site-wide rankings. For weeks, she'd been letting her imagination run wild with ideas of what it would be like to have her first real Valentine's Day with a guy as great as Kenny. What it would be like not to pretend that she wasn't one of those sad, lonely single people on the internet too.

"I don't want you to be alone," he said. "I wanted us to be together."

"I know. It's okay really," she said, hoping he couldn't hear the disappointment in her voice. She had to force herself to look at him. She didn't want him to see how sad she was, but she didn't want him to feel guilty either.

Maya thought she might cry, Kenny looked as sad as she felt.

"You could come with me," he whispered. "We can spend Valentine's Day together, just not doing the thing I planned."

She almost blurted out "YES!" but after San Francisco, she knew she should slow down. "Is it safe?" she asked in a small voice.

"For you, yes. There's been a threat against a foreign diplomat. I'm just there to make sure that it doesn't succeed. It shouldn't be that difficult. And you won't have to be anywhere near him. Actually," he said with a sheepish smile, "Monica kind of told me to keep you as far away from the action as possible. For financial reasons." His words came out in a nervous rush that made Maya want to cry and laugh and touch him.

She blushed at him instead. "So what will I do while you're saving the world?"

He huffed out a small laugh. "The hotel has three pools, a spa, and you can order all the room service you want."

"Oh, count me the fuck in," she exclaimed before he could finish the sentence.

———————————————

three

———————————————

"Oh my god, I feel so fancy," Maya shrieked as she ran her hands over the jet's soft leather chairs. "So much leg room!"

Kenny turned to smile at her as she bounced around in the seat. She was quite possibly the most adorable thing he'd ever seen. He had to pull his attention back to the trip and cargo manifests in his hands. He was going over them with the flight attendant one more time, making sure Kierra had sent along everything he might need. She had. Of course. He skimmed the lists one last time, nodded and used his finger to sign and approve them before handing the tablet over. "Thank you," he said.

"You're welcome, sir. Also, there's a special gift for you and your guest in the bedroom. Courtesy of Ms. Ward."

Kenny nodded but a feeling of apprehension bloomed in his gut. What kind of gifts did Kierra give? Sex toys, his brain screamed as soon as he thought the question. He swallowed nervously.

"We'll be ready for takeoff in just a minute," the flight attendant told him.

He nodded again. When she turned and walked from the main cabin, Kenny took a deep breath before turning to

Maya. His eyes flitted to the far end of the aisle where the door to the bedroom was. Now that he'd been reminded that there was a bed just down the aisle, it was all he could do to keep his mind from conjuring images of crawling into it with Maya. He'd been on this jet too many times to count but being on it with Maya somehow made everything different. God, would there ever be an experience that wasn't improved by her presence alone?

No.

He slid into the seat across from her and smiled. "Do you want something to drink? A magazine?"

"Are you the flight attendant now?"

He reached out and grabbed both of her hands in his. "I just want to make sure you're comfortable."

She moved her legs, entwining them with his, and knocked his right knee with her left. "I'm with you," she whispered. "So I'm very comfortable."

Kenny's cheeks hurt from the smile that spread across his mouth and his face warmed. Maya's smile and blush mirrored his. "This isn't the Valentine's I planned, and I have to work. But I want you to know that every minute I can, I want us to be together. I want the day to be special for us," he said.

She leaned forward and moved her hands to cup his face. "I didn't ever want anything big; just to be with you. As long as we're together, this will be the best Valentine's I've ever had." She frowned, "The bar is the floor actually. The day hasn't even arrived and you've already beat all the other people I've ever dated. Not that it's a competition."

Kenny smiled and raised his eyebrows, "Kierra said something about the Vagina Monologues and your late girlfriend."

"Late *ex*-girlfriend," Maya said and rolled her eyes. "Like I said, the floor."

Kenny closed the distance between their mouths and kissed her, just a taste as the plane began to move. They sat back, buckled their seatbelts and stared at one another as the jet taxied along the runway. They held each other's gazes and Kenny tried not to smile as Maya played footsie with him. He happily failed.

When they were finally at a cruising altitude, Maya began searching around her. "Do these seats recline? This is a long flight."

He gulped and shook his head. "No. There's… um, there's a bedroom."

"What?" She sprang up from her seat and looked back and forth down the aisle before heading toward it.

Kenny was terrified of what Kierra had left them, but he followed Maya with a smile on his face, as entranced by her excitement as ever.

She pushed the door open and shrieked again, "Holy fuck. This is amazing! I'm gonna ride you over the Pacific."

Kenny choked as a blush spread across his neck and face.

She crawled onto the bed and turned onto her back, spreading her arms and legs wide. "So much room," she whispered. "I want to fly like this forever."

He stopped in the doorway to watch her, a bit nervous to cross the threshold.

She turned her head to smile at him. "How could you not tell me there's a bed on this plane?"

"You mean I should have robbed myself of the shock of you promising to ride me over the Pacific?" He chucked, "Nah, couldn't miss that."

She rolled her eyes, "I was always going to promise you that." Her body froze and she sat up in bed. "What's that?"

Kenny's gaze followed the tilt of her head and his heart stopped. The bag looked innocuous enough: shiny and red, with the handles tied together by a large red bow. Kenny's heart stopped as Maya crawled across the bed toward it. She pulled it into her lap. "Is this from you?" she asked, a puzzled smile on her face.

He shook his head.

There was a small card attached and she read it. Her mouth spread into a smile. "To Maya and Kenny. Happy Valentine's Day. KML." She looked up at him. "Aw, my tiny terror can be so sweet."

He nodded and felt his shoulders relax a bit. Maybe it wouldn't be as bad as he was expecting. She patted the bed next to her for him to sit. Their sides were pressed together as she untied the bow. She tilted the bag toward him and he pulled out the red tissue paper, slowly and with bated breath. They both looked into the bag and smiled.

Maya pulled the picture frame out and held it so they could see the image clearly. It was a selfie they'd taken on their extended second date in Hawai'i. "I was actually terrified for a second," she said.

Kenny laughed and nodded. "I was afraid it would be a bag full of condoms and sex toys."

Maya turned to him and whispered, "We don't need Kierra for that."

Kenny rolled his eyes and smiled.

Maya grinned and leaned into him. "Normally I'd kick her ass for breaking into my phone, but this is my favorite picture of us, so I'll just kick her a little bit."

Kenny took the picture from her hands. "That sounds fair. And this is my favorite picture of us too. With clothes."

Maya threw back her head and laughed from deep in her stomach, loud and throaty and one of his favorite sounds in the entire world. His heart swelled.

Later in the flight Maya kept her promise and rode Kenny gently as their plane flew over the Pacific. She put her glasses on the nightstand, crawled on top of him in the darkened cabin and ground her hips into his slowly, softly. The room filled with their gasps and groans. His hands covered her breasts and massaged them as he stared up at her shadowed form. When she was close, he flattened her body against his, their hips moving together and apart with desperate urgency.

He held her face and kissed her almost as slowly as she'd fucked him, tasting her moans, her quivering pussy pulling him over the edge as they came together. She laughed breathlessly into his mouth as he shuddered beneath her and dug his fingers into her waist and pushed up inside her, his body moving of its own greedy volition.

Kenny made sure the blanket covered their naked bodies.

"So what's our cover?" she asked with her head resting on his chest. She sounded sleepy, a gentle slur to her words.

He smiled and kissed the crown of her head. "I own a tech startup and run a charitable foundation. I'm in the country looking for investors and to convince anyone who'll listen that no one needs to be a billionaire. No one needs all of this money."

"I'd absolutely date this very rich nice guy," she said and yawned.

"And I brought my girlfriend along because I'm a workaholic but it's almost Valentine's Day," he finished.

"Mmmm, kinda true, kinda not. Smart."

Kenny chuckled and then yawned himself. "That's what they trained me for."

"So what does a rich philanthropist's kept girlfriend do while her boyfriend is begging for money?"

Kenny chuckled, "Like I said, it's a luxury hotel. You can do whatever you want. Hell, you can spend the entire trip in the spa or-"

"That," Maya barged in quickly. "That's what I'll be doing. Spa and room service while you slip past the security of the richest man in the world and topple a government."

She yawned and turned away from him. He shifted to spoon her, smiling into her shoulder. "I can promise you that I won't be kidnapping the richest man on the planet." He yawned again, "Not on purpose at least."

"So you're going to topple a government," she said and then they fell asleep.

THE TRIP to Hong Kong went by in a flash. Maya woke briefly to deplane and go through customs. She dipped in and out of consciousness in the back of a car, as she watched the water and the lights of the islands come closer and closer and pass them by. By the time they arrived at the hotel, she was exhausted again. She leaned heavily into Kenny's side as he checked them in, steered her to the elevator and into their suite. After the porter left, Kenny undressed her and put her to bed. Her eyes had closed on him sitting at the foot of the bed sorting through a bag full of technology she didn't recognize but knew she couldn't afford to break. She'd woken up in the middle of the night and had to carefully climb out of Kenny's hold to go to the bathroom, his body was wrapped so tightly around her. She'd happily burrowed back into the tangle of his limbs and fallen right back to sleep.

KENNY WOKE up before the sun had risen. Maya's head was resting on his bare chest. He smiled at her soft snoring. He frowned at the sound of his cell phone beeping. When he picked the phone up from the bedside table, the number was encrypted.

He yawned. "Hello," he said into the receiver.

"Rise and shine, Ken Doll. It's time to get to work," Chanté said.

"Give me a second," he said and put the phone back on the table. He pressed a kiss to Maya's forehead and moved her head onto the pillow next to them. He climbed from the bed carefully and grabbed his phone before walking quietly into the sitting area. "Alright, I'm here."

"Did you do some ultra-cute boyfriend shit?" Chanté

asked. "Tell me. Man I wish there were cameras in your room."

"Boundaries, Chanté."

"I said 'I wish,' not that I was installing them. God, calm down. I mean if I had the time… maybe."

"Did you call me for a reason?"

"I am your best friend, Kenneth. Do I need a reason?"

"You need a reason to call *this* phone, actually yes," he huffed out an angry breath.

"Fine, I called because I'm your remote tech support for this mission."

"I know."

"And as your very highly paid tech support, I've pulled together all of the surveillance on the ground for a debrief."

"I'm listening."

"You better be."

He growled into his phone and she laughed.

"So the Prince has been under heavy guard since he arrived. It won't protect him from a really good assassin or a sniper probably, but something is better than nothing."

"How many guards?" Kenny asked. He tilted his head to trap his phone between his ear and shoulder as he kneeled down to open his suitcase of tactical gear.

"I can't be one hundred percent certain but it looks like two personal guards who are with him constantly and a rotating group of at least six others for peripheral hold; one of whom seems to be focused solely on inspecting the Prince's food."

Kenny nodded. "Good."

"Yes and no. Great for keeping most people away, not great for helping you make contact."

Kenny shook his head, even though she couldn't see him, and yawned again. "Contact would be great, but it's not entirely necessary, especially since we don't know who the assassin could be. Better to watch from afar and see who else has their eyes on Prince Mohammed."

He could hear the smile in Chanté's voice. "You're a good spy, Ken Doll."

"Thanks. So the Prince has a public itinerary for this trip," he said. "He's meeting with the emissaries of small countries with large and largely untapped fossil fuel reserves."

"The Nine," Chanté added.

"This is the third of five planned meetings to form a coalition of countries willing to form a unified bloc against Western drilling on their land. Prince Mohammed al Amin has become a bit of a star in the meetings as a progressive and charismatic leader."

"But someone wants him dead?"

"Of course someone wants him dead. He'll succeed his father onto the throne eventually and if he has the same kind of agenda when he's king, he'll probably be damn effective in pulling enough global South states together to provide a legitimate check to Western powers."

"Ah, capitalism and imperialism," Chanté breathed. "Can I be honest?"

"When are you ever not?"

"Good point. I'm a little shocked that *we're* trying to protect him."

Kenny barked out a laugh and cringed. He took his phone from his ear and turned toward the bedroom door, listening for any sign that he'd disturbed Maya. When he didn't hear anything, he put the phone back to his ear.

"Honestly," he said, "I'm a little shocked too. But I'm not going to complain. Since they're ruining my plans, at least it's for something not terrible."

"It's nice to be the good guys this time," Chanté breathed. "Ummm…"

"Okay, it's nice to not be the baddest guys," she offered.

"That's fair. So, here's what I need you to do," he breathed. He pulled the remote tracker from the suitcase and a set of comm earbuds. "I need you to track the Prince's movements in real time and let me know if he goes anywhere odd."

"Uh, I'd love to, but the surveillance I have is delayed at least two hours until the security cameras backup to the hotel's cloud and then I can only see when he's in the hotel's public areas. From what I can tell, he barely goes anywhere or does anything that isn't at the gym or the Summit conference rooms and sometimes the hotel restaurant."

"Great, then this should be easy. I'll get a tracker on him and you can follow him in real time," Kenny said. He moved to the suitcase with his clothing and opened that.

Chanté laughed, "Sorry, didn't you say that you weren't worried about getting close to him? Now you're promising me a tracker?"

He grabbed a pair of running shorts and shoes from his suitcase. "Not on him technically. But I'll get you the next best thing," he said and hung up the phone. He threw his cell on the couch and padded back into the bedroom and through to the bathroom. He took a quick shower, brushed his teeth, and threw a towel around his hips. Maya was still asleep. He opened the drawer on the bedside table, took out the pad of paper and pen and scrawled a quick note.

"Going for a run," he wrote.

It was technically true. Kenny had been pulling together information on Prince Mohammed for months. From what he could tell, the man kept a very strict and surprisingly predictable schedule. He was up just before dawn for prayer, then the gym, then breakfast. Since he'd been in Hong Kong, he was on the elevator at nine in the morning precisely. He rode it down twelve floors to the hotel's main conference rooms for a full day of meetings. He returned to his room for his evening prayers, had dinner – in his room or one of the hotel's restaurants – before an evening workout, the sauna and then he disappeared into his room for the rest of the night. All with a heavy guard shadowing every step. If Kenny wanted even half a chance to get near enough to the Prince – or more importantly his guards – the hotel gym during his morning workout was the best option.

So he brushed another kiss against Maya's forehead. She snorted in her sleep and he smiled against her hair. He walked back into the sitting area and threw on his running shorts, a t-shirt and his running shoes. He slipped the small tracer into a hidden pocket in the waistband of his running shorts and headed out of their suite.

It was time to get to work.

KENNY STEPPED from the elevator onto the hotel's fifth floor, which was dedicated to the gym, sauna, an indoor pool and a whole bunch of other amenities that he would never see. A guard stopped him immediately. Kenny assented to a quick pat down search and gave his cover name and room number. He waited as the guard checked it against the hotel's manifest. He also made sure that he looked confused as he did so. He bypassed the locker room and walked straight into the main part of the gym. He passed another bodyguard at the door and saw two more, one on either side of Prince Mohammed's treadmill.

Kenny made sure not to let his eyes linger on the spectacle of the layers of security the Prince felt necessary just to go for a run in a hotel gym. Instead, he climbed onto his own treadmill a few machines away and began to warm up with a slightly faster than normal walk, then a jog and then a good, steady-paced run.

The trick with most spy-work was to recognize that even though you were pretending to be someone you weren't, you shouldn't pretend to do something you couldn't. It was easier for a mark to recognize that something wasn't right if, for instance, you couldn't breathe correctly through your run. Kenny loved to swim, run, hike and lift weights because they helped him think, so he always made sure to use his need for physical activity as part of his covers. And right now he let himself sink into his current identity.

He looked straight ahead and let his gaze soften, the reflection of the room behind him turning fuzzy as he focused on his breath, his form and his stride; all by feel. He listened to his body and zoned out as he corrected his form and eased into his pace. Once he felt centered, Kenny lifted his eyes and considered the reflection of the room in the mirror. He let his gaze wander left and then right as he normally would. He made eye contact with one of the bodyguards in the mirror by accident. He looked away and continued scanning the room.

The prince's stride began to slow.

Kenny made sure not to give any sign that this mattered. He continued running at the same pace, his eyes roaming in the mirror in front of him as if the Prince's movements didn't matter at all. Because in fact, they didn't. The prince was covered in security. Getting close enough to him to place a tracker would be near impossible. And Kenny should know. Part of his passive surveillance had been to discern any weaknesses in his security. And so far, no matter how he looked at it, the answer had been a resounding no. There was too much security and the Prince was understandably cautious. The only way he'd been able to imagine pulling any information from him would be to place a tracker or transmitter on one of his bodyguards.

Kenny had been considering a tracker as a possibility for increased covert surveillance for almost a month while he'd been working through Prince Mohammed's dossier. He hadn't yet worked out if this was a plausible option in his simulation, but he guessed he'd get his answer sooner rather than later.

The prince stopped jogging and began to walk. Kenny

didn't know how long his slow down would last so he hiked his running shorts up his waist with one hand – surreptitiously retrieving the tracker from the secret compartment – and he reached for his water bottle with the other. He squirted water into his mouth. Swallowed. Squirted another stream into his mouth. Swallowed. And then he moved to put it back in the bottle holder. He feigned a stumble and grabbed the machine to steady himself. His water bottle fell to the ground. Kenny hopped off of the tread onto the sides and paused the machine. As he did so, the Prince spoke to his bodyguard in Arabic. The man moved forward and snatched Kenny's bottle from the ground.

Kenny jumped down from the machine. The bodyguard reached out to hand over his water bottle. Kenny extended both arms in response; one to grab the bottle of water and the other to just lightly touch the other man's elbow. Not enough pressure to be perceived as a threat but enough to attach the tracker, which was thin and small enough not to disrupt the line of his suit and thankfully easily hidden in the dark coat.

"Thank you," Kenny said simply.

The bodyguard eyed him warily but nodded his head slightly.

Kenny turned immediately back to his treadmill and climbed back on. There was no need to linger, in fact that would probably have piqued the guards' suspicion. He carefully put his water bottle back into the holder.

"You should be more careful," Prince Mohammed called to him.

Kenny looked up in the mirror's reflection and smiled easily. "You're not the first person to tell me that." He shrugged.

Mohammed smiled and then turned off his machine.

Kenny turned his machine back on and began to jog slowly. He nodded to the Prince one more time as he and his security filed out of the room. Kenny waited ten minutes, sprinting to get his heart rate going. He slowed his tread to a walk before shutting his machine off.

"Done," he huffed into his ear piece.

"Thank god, that was the most boring thing I've ever sat through," Chanté said in his ear. "Anyway, the tracker stuck. They're back in the Prince's penthouse. I'll let you know if there are any strange movements."

"What about my ground support?"

"Oh yeah. They're in room 1012. But Carlisle wants to meet you for breakfast in an hour and a half."

"You're the best, Chanté."

"Don't give me those cheap compliments," she said. "I like my compliments like I like my glitter: luxurious."

Kenny rolled his eyes. "I'll remember that."

"You better. Now get back up to that suite and give it to our girl good," she purred.

Kenny ripped the ear piece from his ear with a sigh and a shake of his head.

---

four

When Maya woke up, she was alone and a little disoriented. It took a few seconds of staring around the hotel room for her brain fog to clear. She finally started to remember where she was when she grabbed her glasses from the bedside table and pushed them onto her face. She started to reach for her phone to text Kierra, already composing the "Am I out of my mind?" text in her mind because had she really just followed this man halfway around the world just to spend a fake holiday with him? Who the hell was she?

But then she heard the suite's door open. She froze, the blood pumping through her veins felt like a pounding drum in her ears.

Kenny strolled into the room in his socks and a pair of small running shorts. His chest was bare and he'd thrown his shirt over his shoulder. He stopped just inside the room and smiled down at her. "You just wake up?"

She let out the breath she was holding and nodded.

"You're probably thinking 'where the fuck am I?' aren't you?" he asked as he stalked across the room. He threw his shirt onto the floor at the foot of the bed and leaned over her.

Her eyes were wandering all over his body and his bare

skin, glistening with sweat and catching the light streaming through the windows. She nodded absently at his question, only half hearing it. When he leaned over her, though, her brain could only focus on his smell. She bunched the sheets under her in her fist. He smelled like sweat and soap and the faintest trace of her perfume. And apparently that combination did it for her. In a big way. Even though she was half awake and had just been about to freak out that she was apparently falling for this man so quickly, none of that mattered right now. She was suddenly horny as hell.

"You're in Kowloon, Hong Kong with me," he said. He whispered those last two words against her cheek. His mouth trailed across her skin to her ear. "And there's a really big shower in the bathroom," he whispered.

She was crawling out of the bed before he could even finish talking, and he helped her up with a laugh. They pulled her t-shirt over her head as she led the way into the luxury bathroom of her dreams. She was naked in a heartbeat. She turned to look at him over her shoulder, ready to entice him with her best come-hither look, but he beat her to the punch. When they made eye contact, he watched her as he slowly pushed his shorts over his hips. She gasped when his semi-hard dick bounced free.

"You're getting too good at this," she whispered in a breathy moan.

"I'm learning from the best," he said as he followed her into the shower.

Of course she'd followed him halfway around the world, Maya thought to herself. Where the hell else would she rather be?

⬚

MAYA WAS WALKING around the sitting room naked under an unbelted terrycloth robe and Kenny was having a hard time concentrating on tying his tie in the full-length mirror in the corner of the bedroom. His eyes kept wandering from his knot to the reflection of Maya pacing the room, a strawberry from the breakfast he'd ordered in one hand and the spa menu in the other.

She threw the menu on the bed. "Would it be tacky to steal this robe?" Maya asked.

"Yes," Kenny replied. "Please don't do that. I'll buy you a robe."

She sidled up next to him, her naked front pressing into his side. "But I want *this* robe," she whined into his ear.

His face flushed. "Do you know how to tie a tie?" He asked, trying desperately to change the subject.

Her eyebrows furrowed. "Of course I do. I had to teach Jerome for his high school graduation."

He turned to her. "Great. Can you help me out? I can't seem to concentrate," he said as his gaze dipped.

She slithered in between him and the mirror. "Well, when you ask so nicely," she said with a smile.

He watched her as she focused on giving him a simple Windsor knot. She bit her top lip in concentration and he smiled as he slipped his hands into her robe to rest on her bare hips.

She bunched up her nose and shook her head, untying the knot to start again. "I'm rusty," she whispered to herself.

He squeezed her hips reassuringly.

When she'd tied the knot, she exhaled and her mouth spread into a wide, triumphant smile as she looked up at him. "Got it."

Kenny had to stop himself from undoing all of her hard work and taking her back to bed.

She moved out of the way so he could examine his tie in the mirror. It was perfect. But it could have been terrible and he still would have loved it. He turned to her and dug his fingers into her braids, pulling her mouth to his. The kiss was quick but hard. He sucked her bottom lip into his mouth and let it fall from his lips.

She smiled against his mouth. "Wait 'til you find out that I know how to mend a button."

He licked the curve of her lips and spoke against her mouth. "Don't tell me that yet. I can't handle it. Come on, let's get you dressed before I leave." He felt her shiver against him.

He took one of her hands and led her to the bed.

"Do you have time for this?" she asked.

"I'm making time."

Her very neatly organized suitcase was open on the floor near the closet. His hands moved right to the small mesh bag where she'd packed all of her lingerie. He set the bag on the bed and turned to her. She licked her lips nervously and peeled off the robe.

He let his eyes wander over her body – slightly flushed from the shower and her rising lust – for a few seconds. He put the bag on the bed and rummaged through it until he found his favorite pair of light brown lace underwear and matching bra. The color matched her skin tone almost perfectly. He sat on the bed and opened his legs for her. She stepped tentatively between his spread limbs. Her breasts were right in front of his face. He wanted to taste her again. Like always. But he waited until she brought her hands up to his shoulders.

He kissed one nipple. "I want you to enjoy yourself at the spa today," he whispered against her breast.

He could feel her nod and release a breathy moan.

He kissed her other nipple. He leaned slightly forward, positioning her underwear so that she could step into them, using his shoulders to keep her stable. They both held their breath as he pulled the delicate scrap of material up her legs.

Her hands moved to his head, nails scraping along his scalp, as she spread her thighs for him. He smoothed her underwear into place and then brushed his mouth over the curve of her belly. She moaned.

He looked up at her. "Turn around, sweetheart," he whispered against her left breast, his tongue following his words.

She nodded absently as she did so.

He had to take a deep breath before he could reach for the matching bra. He stood and wrapped his arms around her so she could put her arms through the straps. They positioned the bra onto her chest and she adjusted her breasts in the cups. He waited until she nodded to clasp it in place. He sat back on the bed, pulled her to him and bent forward to kiss each of the soft rolls of flesh at her sides.

She laughed.

He smiled against her skin.

When he stood, he wrapped himself around her and walked her back in front of the full-length mirror. "I'll come find you in the spa when I'm done," he said to her reflection.

"What's my limit? This place can't be cheap."

His hands roamed up and down her arms and then over her stomach. He shook his head, "No limit. Do whatever you want."

She lifted an eyebrow. "You giving me permission to bankrupt you?"

"Absolutely," he whispered into her ear as his right hand dipped into the front of her underwear.

Her head fell back and she gasped as his left hand slid down the back of her underwear. "Oh fuck," she breathed.

He flattened the pads of two fingers against her clit and moved in gentle circles, while two fingers from his other hand pushed down the crack of her ass, through her thighs and into her pussy.

She spread her legs wider and her eyes drifted closed as he stroked her.

"I want you to watch, Maya," he whispered.

She groaned again, but lifted her head and opened her eyes.

He hardly knew where to look himself. That was one of the best things about Maya. There was always so much beauty to see no matter where he looked. But eventually his gaze settled on his arm disappearing into her underwear, his hands moving in increasingly fast circles over her clit and in her sex. Kenny began to unconsciously thrust his hips against her as her soft, warm, wet sex engulfed his fingers and clenched down on his digits as he pumped them in and out.

"Oh fuck," she hissed. She grabbed his right wrist, not to stop him, but to urge him on.

He turned his head and brought his mouth to her ear. "You ready to come?"

She shivered and let out a choked moan that almost sounded like a yes.

He pushed a third finger into her cunt and increased the pressure on her clit. She gasped and laughed at the same time and then came all over his left hand with a shuddering groan and shaking thighs.

His hands slowed and eventually stilled. He didn't need to check his watch to know that he needed to head out soon. Very soon. But he hadn't been lying to Monica. The mission wasn't as important as Maya. So he held her until her body stopped quaking. When she was calm, he walked her back to bed and opened the covers for her to climb under. He left her for a moment to wash his hands and straighten his tie. He kissed her and whispered sweet words and dirty promises to her as she drifted back to sleep.

He might have to rush a bit; take the stairs rather than wait for the elevator. But he'd make it to his breakfast meeting in time. And he'd do what he always did when he left her for work. He'd use the memory of Maya coming in his arms and his own desire to get back to her as the motivation he needed to handle this job as quickly as possible.

———————————————

five

———————————————

"Michael Zhang, Michael Zhang, Michael Zhang," Maya mumbled quietly to herself in the elevator on the way down to the hotel spa.

In the past few months Maya had been surprised to find that dating a spy was actually quite normal. Sure, sometimes he disappeared in the middle of the night with a cryptic good-bye. And yeah okay, he called her from a blocked number because his cell number was classified. But she'd gotten used to not asking him where he was *exactly* or when he was coming home, much faster than she might have expected. She'd been in a lot of relationships with people who'd been less than honest. At least Kenny's cryptic answers made actual sense. Besides, Kenny's evasiveness about the particulars of his job were understandable and easy to bear when compared to his almost embarrassing honesty about everything else.

It was a heady rush. *He* was a heady rush. Everything about being with Kenny had been unexpected and lovely and surprising and fun; a combination of things Maya hadn't been sure she would experience again and certainly not in a relationship. But now that she had it, she didn't want to mess it up, and she was kind of terrified that she would. Because it was one thing to keep a firm hold about what she could and could not know about Kenny, and an entirely other thing to keep his cover identity straight in her head.

So he wasn't Kenny or, when she wanted to needle him, Ken Doll. While they were on this trip – er, mission – he had to be Mr. Zhang or Michael. And she was his spoiled girlfriend, Candy. Candy! She was going to kill Kierra when she saw her.

The elevator stopped on the third floor and the doors slid open to reveal a luxurious and calming reception room. Everything was bamboo and warm browns with pops of soothing cream. Everything looked expensive. Too expensive for Maya. But not, she thought to herself as she stepped tentatively off of the elevator, for Candy, girlfriend of millionaire international financier and philanthropist, Mr. Michael Zhang. She took a deep breath and straightened her back. Yeah, this was all right up Candy's alley.

"Hello," a woman said as she stepped from behind the front desk. "Do you have an appointment?"

And just like that, Maya was Maya again, not Candy. She didn't know she needed an appointment. "Um... no but-"

"I'm sorry," the woman frowned politely, "but you must have an appointment. Would you like to make one? We are booked for the next few weeks, however."

Maya sighed. She'd really wanted a massage. She'd been working long days planning and pre-recording special Valentine's content for her ChatBot channel and other social media so she and Kenny could have the day together without any interruptions. And even though the date he'd planned was interrupted, she thought the least she could do was be pampered while he was out doing spy stuff. But apparently she wasn't even going to get that. She shook her head and sighed again. "I won't be here in a few weeks."

The woman frowned at her with soft, sympathetic eyes.

"Maybe we can fit you in for a short neck massage," she said kindly.

She walked back to the reception desk. "What is your room number?"

There was a siren blaring in Maya's head that reminded her to say, "I'm in the Garden Penthouse. With Mr. Zhang."

The woman raised her head, a wide smile on her face. "Ah, why didn't you say so? Mr. Zhang called ahead."

Maya started, "He what now?"

"He has booked you in for an all-day retreat."

"He *what* now?"

"Full body massage, facial massage and steam, mud bath and detox, manicure and pedicure, lunch in between of course."

"He-" Maya couldn't even finish her question. Her mouth fell open and tears sprang to her eyes. "Oh my god, he's perfect," she whispered.

"Yes," the woman said, leaning toward her on a whisper. "Considerate, rich *and* handsome, I hear. You are truly lucky."

Maya could feel the blush warming her face as a single tear slipped from her right eye. She nodded. "I know," she croaked. "Believe me, I know."

▭

A YEAR AGO, Kenny would have spent every waking moment preparing for a new mission. He would have used his travel time to get knee-deep in dossiers and directives and contingency plans. A year ago, Kenny would have disconnected from his entire life – barren as it was – to prepare to do his job with a singular focus. But he was a different person today. Kenny's day or so of prep time had been spent on the plane between Maya's legs, in the hotel room between Maya's legs and dreaming about being between Maya's legs. A year ago, he would have felt terrible that he was so underprepared, but so much had changed that he couldn't even make himself care. Besides, he reminded himself, Monica and Lane had sprung this mission on him at the literal last minute. So he'd get the job done, but it wouldn't be elegant. He didn't have elegance to spare.

On the mezzanine, he walked from the elevator to the hotel restaurant. He gave his name to the maître d'.

"Hello sir. Your guest has already arrived."

Kenny nodded in return and followed the man through the restaurant.

Carlisle was sitting at a table nearest the large wall of windows at the far end of the restaurant. Kenny could see the city's skyline in the background, with the shore and docks beyond. As he neared, he realized that the windows also overlooked the outdoor pool. A few people were lounging around it, but the water was still and clear. As he neared, Carlisle stood and extended his arm. They shook hands politely, like business partners, which was technically true.

The maître d' placed their menus in front of them and only left when a waiter appeared at his side. They each ordered blindly, anything to get the waiter away and quickly.

"What's your report?" Kenny whispered to Carlisle once they were alone.

"The day's Summit meetings have started. Security for the Prince and all the other diplomats is high. They're everywhere."

"Do you think they know about the threat?"

Carlisle sat back in his chair and seemed to really consider the question. "It's hard to tell. Prince Mohammed always has a lot of security." He tilted his head down and then smirked, "And they are none too friendly when you *accidentally* press the wrong button and show up on the eighth floor looking for the buffet."

Kenny smiled. "So I guess we're not busting into the summit."

The other man shook his head. "I've embedded one of my men in the wait staff though. He's pissed, so if you want to take his place…?"

Kenny raised a haughty eyebrow. Serve world leaders canapés while Maya had half a suitcase of lingerie? "Absolutely not."

Carlisle shrugged. "So what's the plan? Monica said you'd have a plan." He leaned forward and grabbed his glass of water. He took a slow sip. "A good one," he added many seconds later.

"No pressure," Kenny mumbled to himself. He took a deep breath as he settled into the cover he'd decided to use. "Alright, I've checked into the hotel under an alias I've been developing as part of a global philanthropic movement," Kenny said as he leaned back in his chair, casually, to detail his plan. He was immeasurably happy that it sounded much more plausible out loud than he'd imagined. "I built the cover for another mission, but it still holds water. The Prince's security will have already run a check on my identity by now."

"So the plan is to just… wait until he decides your cover is interesting enough to talk to?" Carlisle arched a skeptical eyebrow at him.

"If we had time, maybe. But we don't have time. This morning I crashed the Prince's workout to force a background check but also to place a tracker on one of his bodyguards."

"Why? So far as we know, the man hasn't left the hotel since he checked in."

"So far as we know. There's also a chance that this might be an inside job, it can't hurt to get even a little more intel. Monica always says that no matter how good the prior intel or prep time, we always know less than we think."

Carlisle nodded and considered his words. "Okay, what if he does a security check and he doesn't want to meet you?"

Kenny shrugged. "That's fine. I don't want to be his best friend. All I want to do is make sure that he and his bodyguards don't look twice at me when they see me around the hotel so I can blend into the background and see who else is trying to do the same."

Carlisle smiled at him. "You just might be better than she promised."

Unlike Chanté or Maya, Kenny did not speak compliment as a first language. They could fluster him, especially when they came secondhand and even more so when they came from Monica. He couldn't handle that. So he pushed it aside and focused on the mission.

They both turned as the maître d' sidled up next to their table. He had a silver tray in one hand with a piece of paper atop it. "Excuse me, sir," he whispered, leaning toward Kenny. "I'm sorry to interrupt, but I have a message for you."

"Who's it from?" Kenny asked with a bored expression on his face even though his heart had sped up.

Instead of answering, the maître d' extended his arm for Kenny to pluck the note from the tray. He did and nodded. The maître d' turned and walked away.

Kenny held his breath as he opened the note. He wouldn't smile. He was a better agent than that. But he did read the short note twice to confirm its message.

"You wanna share with the class?" Carlisle breathed.

Kenny handed the note to Carlisle across the table. The other man read it aloud.

"Dear Mr. Zhang-
After running into you in the gym, my security team ran a
background check on you. I hope you will understand and
forgive my caution. As you may or may not know, I am
meeting with representatives from smaller oil-rich countries
from all over the world. Considering your philanthropic work,
I feel certain that our meeting was not a coincidence. You
have my attention. Please join the Summit members tonight

for drinks. And of course, you may bring your companion. I look forward to your proposal."

CARLISLE HANDED THE NOTE BACK. "Do you have a proposal?"

Kenny smiled, "I will by tonight."

Carlisle smiled. "I hear you brought Kierra's roommate with you."

Kenny's back stiffened. "I did."

Carlisle leaned forward and whispered, "Would it be weird to ask for an autograph?"

Kenny exhaled loudly and rolled his eyes. "Yes."

"Lane said you'd say that. I'm still gonna do it."

Kenny squinted at Carlisle across the table. "You seem to be having a lot of conversations with Monica and Lane-"

"And Kierra," Carlisle said and licked his lips. "Can't forget her."

Kenny was about to ask a question, but the dirty and wistful gleam in Carlisle's eyes gave him the only answer he needed. Whatever Carlisle was into with his bosses and Maya's best friend wasn't work related. It was personal. And none of his business. He stood from the table. "I'll be in touch," he said.

Carlisle nodded up at him as his smile broadened. "You should consider a mask," he said.

Kenny frowned. "What?"

"A mask. Next time you're on Maya's channel. If you wear a mask you could increase your filming angles."

He rolled his eyes. "Does everyone watch our broadcasts?"

Carlisle stood and walked around the table. He reached out to straighten Kenny's tie, which was almost certainly not crooked. "You're like an Agency celebrity. And we support our own. See you tonight." He winked and then turned to walk away.

Kenny rolled his eyes and watched the other man go.

He snatched the Prince's note from the table, put it into his jacket pocket and went off in search of Maya. He hadn't expected that this would be a lesson Monica would teach him but learning to make use of his downtime was more important than he'd ever realized. It was punctuated at Command by the sudden slamming of an office door, the sound of Kierra's giggling moans from just around the corner and sometimes — when things were slow and he could close and lock his own office door — the sound of Maya's laughter as she answered his frantic FaceTime call in the middle of the day for a quick bit of phone sex.

No spy could be on all the time.

▭

TECHNICALLY VALENTINE'S Day was tomorrow. And technically this spa trip was part of Kenny's cover — maybe, Maya wasn't one hundred percent sure. Oh, and also the bar really was the floor as far as all of her romantic Valentine's Days before this one. But Maya felt certain that this was the absolute best Valentine's Day of her life. How could it not be? How could Kenny or anyone beat this, she wondered to herself with a sigh — one of many — as she reclined on an ergonomic couch in the spa's "recovery room."

She was snuggled in the softest terrycloth robe she'd ever felt, softer even than the one she was considering stealing in their suite. Her toes and nails were freshly painted and her entire body felt like what a slab of ribs probably felt like the night before a barbecue. Every muscle was soft and relaxed and had been kneaded and rubbed into submission. She closed her eyes and smiled happily to herself. Seriously, best Valentine's of her life. And she was going to make sure that

Kenny had the best Valentine's Day of his life starting tonight, just as soon as she woke up from her nap, she thought, as she drifted off to sleep.

She didn't quite make it to unconsciousness, however. The door to the recovery room opened on a whisper. Maya opened one eye to peek at the person walking quietly in. She was tall, covered – as Maya was – in white terrycloth, which contrasted nicely with her rich, dark brown skin. Her face was smooth and unlined. She looked older and sophisticated but friendly. Maya opened her other eye and smiled up at her.

The other woman's face lit up with an answering smile as she sank into one of the other couches. "Hello," she whispered.

"Hi," Maya whispered back.

"Don't let me interrupt you."

Maya nodded and rested her head back onto her chair. It took a while, but she recaptured that freshly-rubbed-down-slab-of-ribs feeling again and drifted off to sleep with thoughts of Kenny's Valentine's Day presents on her mind.

She woke with a start when someone put a hand on her shoulder.

"Calm down. It's just me," Kenny said, his hands gripping her arms tight to anchor her.

"You scared me," she said, groggy with sleep and relaxation, her eyes closing again.

"I'm sorry. I didn't want to wake you but…"

She lifted one eyebrow. "But what?"

"I told you I'd come find you when I was done," he whispered.

Her heavy eyelids opened, and she shimmied to sit up.

His hands fell to the chair on either side of her thighs and he leaned forward.

Her eyes darted to the other chaise. The woman with the great skin was gone.

"Did you bring anything dressy? Formal?"

She squinted at him. "I mostly packed lingerie and sex toys."

His laughter filled the bright, quiet room. "Of course you did."

"But…" she whispered, drawing his attention to her mouth. "I did bring this dress."

"I'm listening," he whispered back.

He watched with rapt attention as she sucked her bottom lip into her mouth. His eyes glazed over in lust.

"I wanted to be prepared," she whispered. "Just in case you had a special dinner planned." She leaned forward, "Did you have a special dinner planned for me, babe?"

His eyes darted to hers and he grinned, "I'm still not telling. But how do you feel about being my arm candy at a diplomatic event tonight?"

She smoothed her hand over the front of his shirt. "I'm *always* your arm candy, babe."

He dipped his head to kiss her softly. "Yes, you are," he whispered against her lips. He sat back and lifted his eyebrows, "Do you want to stay or go back upstairs?"

She pretended to think through those options. "Let's go upstairs. I want to thank you for the best massage of my life."

"This was Kierra's idea actually. She and Chanté did all the work," he said.

"Well, I'm not gonna thank either of them the way I'm about to thank you, that's for sure."

Kenny blushed Maya's favorite shade of red. He leaned forward to kiss her deeply, laughing against her mouth. The only thing that stopped them from reclining onto the chaise lounge was an attendant bringing in another client. Were it not for that, Maya would have pushed Kenny onto a chaise and recovered from her spa treatments in an entirely different way.

"ANYTHING HAPPEN on the tracker I put on the body-guard?" Kenny asked Chanté. He was multi-tasking in the sitting room, shining his shoes and debriefing with Chanté while he waited for Maya to finish "creating a masterpiece" – or, in other words, getting dressed.

"Nothing," Chanté said. "He was in the conference area all day. Carlisle's man said he was fighting with the Kuwaiti minister for a bit, but it was just about tariffs. Super boring. When they broke for lunch, the Prince's bodyguard went to his suite and he's there now. I presume with the Prince, but since the tracker's not on him I can't be sure. So you're bringing Maya tonight?" she asked excitedly.

"Only because the Prince knows she's here. If I could have avoided that, I would."

"Don't worry, Ken Doll. My girl knows how to handle herself. She'll be fine."

Kenny's fear felt like a piece of lead in his stomach. Bringing Maya to Hong Kong, he could do. Letting Maya loose in the luxury hotel's wellness spa was more than fine. But the idea of ushering her right into the orbit of danger would never sit well with him. So he tried not to think about it.

"I want you coordinating with Carlisle to scan the room and flag anyone who shouldn't be at the Summit."

"Yeah yeah, I know the drill," Chanté whined. Chanté never whined.

"What's going on with you?"

She exhaled dramatically. "Nothing. I'm fine."

She wasn't fine. Kenny could see that. "Where are you?"

"Oooh, sorry," she shook her head, "I can't share that information. I don't want a certain tall, dark, and handsome spy to know."

"And you think *I* would tell him?"

"Of course not, but he's getting a little… desperate so I need to be careful," she replied.

"Chanté seriously, what's going on? Is there something I

need to know? Do you need me to shoot him?" Kenny couldn't keep the glee from his voice at that last question.

Chanté was trying to hide her smile. She pursed her lips and it only made her large cheeks puff out even more. It was adorable. "He's never chased *me* before," she whispered, leaning closer to her computer's camera, her dark eyes dancing. "For almost a decade I've been chasing him or waiting for him or running to him. But now he's…"

"He misses you," Kenny finished her sentence.

She nodded excitedly.

"Chanté, that's not healthy," he said in a gentle voice. "I know I'm not one to talk about less than stellar relationship dynamics or relationships in general, but it shouldn't be a game where you trade your pain back and forth. You know that, right?"

Her head dipped forward. He watched as she swiped a hand across one cheek. When she raised her head, Kenny was angry at himself for wiping that big-cheeked happiness from her face. But what kind of best friend would he be if he didn't say anything?

She tried to smile but couldn't. "Can we talk about something else?" she whispered.

He nodded. "But if you ever need to talk…" he said, not needing to finish the sentence.

This time she managed a smile in response. It was small and sad, but genuine.

"How do I look?" Maya called just before she stepped into the sitting room. The black velvet halter dress she wore was floor-length and hugged every curve of her body.

Kenny felt as if the temperature of the room had risen by more than a few degrees.

"I wanna see!" Chanté yelled back, her face lighting up again.

Maya's steps faltered and she frowned.

Kenny turned his laptop toward her.

She leaned forward, "Chanté?"

"Hubba hubba. Hellooooo cleavage," Chanté replied.

Kenny rolled his eyes and turned the laptop back to him.

"Boo, I wanna see the lady," Chanté yelled. Maya giggled and fell onto the couch next to him.

Kenny tried not to notice the way her breasts bounced in the deep-v neckline. He failed. She winked at him knowingly.

Maya turned to the laptop. "Hey Chanté," she trilled.

"Hello, doll face. I love this dress and makeup and hair!"

Maya patted the high bun she'd twisted her braids into on top of her head. Kenny thought it made her look regal. Even more than normal. "You know, I try. What are you up to, short stuff?"

"Ah you know, the same. Hacking into a bank in the Seychelles. Tracking this Prince so Kenny can stop him from being killed."

"Chanté," Kenny hissed.

"And looking for some new music for my next residency," she continued as if Kenny hadn't interrupted her.

"Where are you going next?"

"Oooh sorry. Can't share that info quite yet."

Maya nodded, "You still hiding from that fine man with all that gorgeous ass hair?"

"Excuse me?" Kenny turned toward Maya.

He saw her eyes flit his way before she spoke. "His dick must be bomb," she whispered. "Oh my god, babe," she laughed as Kenny pulled her onto his lap. "I was just playing." She lifted her dress to straddle his lap. He reached a hand up to cup the back of her head gently, not wanting to disturb her hair or makeup.

She smiled down at him. "I was just playing, babe," she laughed. She ran her hands over his head.

He closed his eyes as the pleasure of her touch radiated from the crown of his head down his body.

She leaned forward and whispered into his ear, "Yours is the only bomb dick that matters to me. You know that."

He smiled and opened his eyes. Her beautiful brown eyes flashed with happiness and he felt those words somewhere deep in his chest. He wanted to give her his Valentine's Day gift right now. It was early, but suddenly he didn't want to wait. The sound of the video call ending caught their attention. They both turned to the computer just as his cell phone chimed.

Maya leaned back to pluck it from the coffee table and hand it over. He opened his messages. "It's Chanté. She said she got called away." He sighed. "She also said your ass looks great in this dress."

Maya smiled and ran her hands over her hair. "The girl's got taste."

"So, are you ready to go charm the pants off of some rich politicians?" he asked, gripping her waist briefly.

"I'm ready to eat lots of hors d'oeuvres and drink champagne while you charm the pants off some rich politicians, yes."

"Sounds like a plan," he laughed as she climbed off his lap.

"You look beautiful," he said and offered his hand to her.

She smiled and laced her fingers with his. "You look pretty great, yourself."

"Yeah?"

She nodded and smirked, "Who's the arm candy now?"

---

six

Maya had skipped lunch. She hadn't meant to. She didn't believe in that. Bodies needed fuel. But apparently her body had been so happy at being rubbed and scrubbed and massaged into oblivion that her stomach had completely checked out until she saw a tray of puff pastries filled with something that smelled oniony and rich heading away from her.

She turned to Kenny and kissed him on the cheek quickly. "Good luck saving the world," she breathed and then she was off.

"Candy," he called after her.

She raised a hand and waved goodbye to him. She made eye contact with a waiter and gave him her best smile. His mouth went slack, and he stopped in his tracks. Exactly what she wanted. She grabbed two puff pastries from his tray and headed off in search of a drink. With a savory tartelette in one hand and a glass of champagne in the other she finally turned to survey the room.

The crowd was mostly men and she rolled her eyes at that. She could easily identify the politicians and political aides by their very boring suits in gray or black. Then there were the

Prince's bodyguards, in their dark black suits. She could tell them apart by their very conspicuous earpieces. And the bulge of their shoulder holsters. And then there was the Prince himself. Even if Chanté hadn't let it slip that he was royalty, Maya would have known. He sat at a table by himself, surrounded by security, looking out at the room as if it was all beneath him. He was also the only man not in a suit. Instead he wore a thawb, which Maya was completely shocked to realize she knew the word for. Apparently that elective on Arab societies and cultures in her last semester at college had actually taught her something, regardless of that C she'd earned.

She watched as a bodyguard led Kenny toward the Prince, another patted him down and then yet another led him to the Prince's table. Maya shadowed their movements, grabbing a fruit skewer on the way. She knew that Kenny would want her to stay close and visible. And she also wanted to keep an eye on him. It was only a happy coincidence that the tall table where she parked herself was right outside of the swinging doors that led to the kitchen. She was in the direct path of the waiters and Kenny. Truly, being a spy didn't seem that hard.

She smiled so wide that a waitress coming through the door tripped and Maya gasped. But the woman was a professional and managed to keep the tray level and recover. Maya didn't want to draw attention to her, but she smiled and gave the waitress two thumbs up. The waitress smiled back and walked toward her.

Maya happily accepted the satay and waved as the waitress walked away. The poor girl only looked back at Maya twice.

"Here you are again."

Maya turned toward the voice, mid-bite, and her eyes lit up. She chewed happily and pointed at her mouth. The pretty older woman from the spa set her wine glass on the table between them.

"Hi," Maya swallowed and said. But then she frowned.

"My name is Rita," the woman said, offering her hand.

Maya shook her head and smiled. "I'm Candy," she said, happy that she didn't cringe at the terrible fake name.

"Funny running into you here," Rita said.

"I know. Although I guess if you don't leave the hotel, then it's easy to meet the same people."

Rita nodded. "Are you here with your husband?"

Maya blushed and shook her head. "Boyfriend. I tagged along for a work trip. Valentine's Day." She rolled her eyes, feigning annoyance.

Rita's smile seemed to soften. "That's lovely."

"No, it's corny. It's just a made-up holiday."

"It is, but…" Maya watched as Rita's attention seemed to drift away. Her smile dipped into a frown but only briefly. She recovered and focused back on Maya. "It might be made up, but if your relationship is real… every moment together is worth it."

"That's beautiful. And kinda sad," Maya said.

"Life tends to be that way, I've found."

There was something so heartbreaking in the half-smile on Rita's face. Maya wanted to comfort her and run away from whatever made her words sound so haunted. "Are you here with someone?"

Rita's smile widened, but her eyes were still deep, dark pools. "A business associate. I tagged along as support staff."

Maya couldn't help but look Rita up and down. The slim, pinstriped pantsuit fit her body like a glove. "You're the best-looking support staff in this room."

Rita laughed. "I like you, Candy."

"I hear I'm likeable."

"I believe that," she replied just as the waitress from before returned with a tray.

Maya grabbed another satay. "Thank you," she gushed. The waitress smiled shyly as she walked away. And then another waiter arrived with a tray of champagne. Maya grabbed another and smiled at him as well.

"It seems that you might be more than likable," Rita said. "Your boyfriend has his work cut out for him."

Maya's eyes wandered to Kenny. He was leaning forward, speaking passionately to the Prince. His face was flushed, and his ears looked adorable. "Nah. He's got absolutely nothing to worry about," Maya whispered with a soft smile playing at her lips.

▭

MAYA WAS NOT PLAYING. As soon as they'd walked into the small ballroom on the eighth floor, she'd brushed a kiss to Kenny's cheek and then followed after a waiter without a second glance.

"Good luck saving the world," she'd whispered before abandoning him.

Kenny wanted to follow her and make sure that she stayed right by his side. But actually, he realized as soon as one of Prince Mohammed's bodyguards came to fetch him, this was for the best. As if she knew that he would be anxious, she made sure to stay in his line of sight and as usually happened, the room seemed to orbit around her. She was close to the door leading to the kitchen and seemed to have charmed all the waiters into giving her first pick of each new dish and making sure she had a fresh glass of champagne when she needed it. Maya looked like she was in heaven. Kenny was focused on the mission, but he never let her out of his peripheral vision.

"Please, Mr. Zhang," Prince Mohammed said. "Let us get to business. Our meeting here was not a coincidence, yes?"

Kenny smiled affably, "No, it wasn't."

"I am assuming that you have a proposal for me?" The Prince sounded… tired. That was an unexpected realization.

In the split second he had to consider his answer, Kenny's brain sifted through every bit of intel he'd read over the past few months. Mohammed was the eldest son of the current king of Qatar. His family had ruled the country for almost ninety years. His father's efforts at modernization had been frustrated not by legitimate democratic disagreements in the country, but always, time and again, by outside interference. He had been educated in England, Germany and China and had been, for the past two years, shadowing the Qatari foreign minister to the US. No one who had been watching him or his father closely for any amount of time was shocked when he called for this oil summit. Kenny had taken more than his fair share of world history and global politics courses to know that this was a great idea with only a sliver of a chance of actually succeeding. But he admired Mohammed's effort.

And he was damn shocked to find himself here trying to *stop* someone from killing him.

But he knew all of this already.

Maya moved in his peripheral vision and he turned his head involuntarily, just needing to check in on her. One of the waitresses had parked herself in front of Maya and the two were chatting like old friends, sharing the hors d'oeuvres on the tray in between them. Kenny smiled. And then he remembered something and turned back to the Qatari royal.

"Your sister had a rare form of leukemia, yes?" he asked carefully.

The other man sat up straighter and Kenny watched his fists clench.

"I don't mean to pry or be insensitive. But I remember reading about it at university."

He took a deep breath through his nose and nodded tersely.

"She needed a special treatment that she could only get in the US. But she was denied a visa to travel. Even with all of your money and influence. Even though the US has been buying oil from your country for decades at incredibly favorable prices. Your sister was denied a visa because of a war in a neighboring country."

Kenny watched as every part of Prince Mohammed's body became ever tighter with tension as he spoke.

"She died in a hospital waiting as you appealed for medical relief. I'm sure she had the best care available and her doctors made her as comfortable as they could. But she still died. If this could happen to her, then it could happen to anyone. Even worse, what if the closest hospital is two days' walk away? And what if that hospital has one overworked doctor and a handful of equally overworked nurses and a larger handful of untrained volunteers? And what if the entire facility was full of out of date equipment? What if that hospital was in the middle of a war zone? What if that hospital *was* a war zone?

I know the Summit is about freeing your countries from Western control, but what's the point of all that if your people are still destitute? If they can't access good healthcare or jobs or even clean water? I'm here, Your Highness, because I want to convince you that you shouldn't just be working to free yourself from the shackles of Western interference. You should be freeing your people from the shackles of poverty."

Kenny had leaned forward, his eyes boring into Prince Mohammed's. His face was warm and his skin was tingling. He meant every word he'd said.

The Prince considered him for a long, silent moment. He worked hard to unclench his fists, one by one. He took in many fortifying breaths. "Why are you here telling *me* this? You are American, right?"

Kenny frowned, "I am."

"Then why not tell your countrymen this?"

"I have. I will continue to. I also know that my likelihood of success is low at the moment. Making politicians care about poor people they either can't see or don't want to see and a system that makes it possible for them to be reelected over and over again for their ignorance… that's a different battle.

But this entire summit is based on the idea that your countries aren't like the West, yes? You want to be better if given the freedom to do so. Let's say you succeed," Kenny said, sitting back in his chair and crossing his legs. "Let's say you create your Near East oil bloc and you manage to raise the price of your oil and exert some international pressure. Where will that money go, Your Highness? Into your overseas bank accounts? To buy another home for your family in Europe? Or will you re-build the schools that the Russian-led forces destroyed in the last war? Will you open more hospitals? Will you send young doctors to the West to train so that the next person in your country born with the same rare disease that killed your sister has a different fate? Will you do what it takes so that child's family doesn't have to watch their loved one die, not even able to afford the hope of a visa? I know my country's history. *That* would make you better than us."

Prince Mohammed considered Kenny and his words before nodding tersely and standing from his chair. Kenny rose as well. "I will give your proposal some thought. In the meantime, please enjoy the refreshments with your…" His head turned to Maya who had managed to rope yet another woman into her orbit.

"Fiancée," Kenny said automatically. He didn't need to think about that for even a millisecond. "Or at least she will be soon."

"Congratulations," Prince Mohammed said before turning and walking away, his bodyguards trailing behind him.

"Croquette, sir?" a voice said to his left.

He turned and raised an eyebrow at Carlisle. "I'd think this," he said gesturing toward his waiter's uniform, "would be beneath you."

Carlisle lifted the tray closer to Kenny and didn't speak until he'd taken an appetizer. "I'm not above doing whatever's necessary to get the job done. For instance, I've got a tracker on the Prince's car just in case he leaves the hotel. And thanks to your extended conversation with the Prince and your girlfriend over there sucking up all the air in the room-"

"It's her gift," Kenny said.

"You two distracted the Prince's bodyguards long enough that I could hover close and your hacker got into one of their cell phones."

Kenny couldn't help but smile. "Sounds like this was a successful op."

Carlisle lifted an eyebrow. "We'll see. Meanwhile, you might want to go check in on your girlfriend. I heard one of the waitresses talk about proposing."

Kenny turned to Maya as Carlisle walked away. And sure enough, she was surrounded by a few more waiters, the bartender had abandoned his post and the Nigerian finance minister was inching closer to her side each second. Kenny had to elbow his way to her.

"Hey babe," she said around a satay stick. "Did you try the chicken?"

He shook his head with a smile, "I didn't. We can leave if you want." Kenny didn't have to turn around to feel the tension as they all waited for her answer.

But Maya's eyes hadn't left his since he walked up to her. She smiled and bit her bottom lip as she nodded emphatically. "Yes, please," she purred. Someone behind him groaned.

Kenny took her hand and pulled her through the crowd. He made the briefest moment of eye contact with Carlisle and before he knew it, they were back in the elevator heading to their room.

He pushed her into the corner of the elevator and kissed her jaw. "Did you have fun?"

She grabbed his left hand and moved it under the hem of her dress. "Yes," she whispered as his fingers traced the soft crease of her thighs.

His mouth moved across her cheek and then he looked at her, their mouths so close.

"Did you do what you needed to do?" she asked.

He nodded.

"Does that mean you're all mine for the rest of the night?" Her breath hitched as he pushed his hand between her thighs and cupped her mound. She closed her eyes and smiled.

"I'm all yours for as long as you want me."

"You always say the sweetest things just before you fuck me dirty," she said.

He dipped his head to suck her bottom lip into his mouth in answer.

She cupped his head and pulled him closer. The kiss was desperate as if they had been separated for longer than maybe half an hour. Her tongue stroked his forcefully and he welcomed it, sucking it into his mouth.

She laughed as he hooked two fingers around her underwear and stroked her wet lips.

"Are you always going to be this wet for me?" he mumbled against her mouth.

She nipped at his mouth, "If you look this good in a suit and whisk me out of parties to get me off in an elevator, you can count on it."

The elevator stopped moving and dinged as the doors opened. They pulled away from one another and sped down the short hallway to their hotel room.

As Kenny fumbled with the key to the door Maya draped herself over his back and whispered in his ear, "It's almost Valentine's Day."

He unlocked the door and stepped inside. He was horny, but not horny enough not to flick the lights on and scan the room, checking to make sure nothing looked out of place. He'd set a perimeter alarm so he'd have known if someone had come even close to their door, but he could never be too cautious. Not where Maya was concerned. He felt her frenetic energy at his back. She waited excitedly, but patiently, for him to scan the sitting room and then the bedroom and bathroom.

"Clear," he called to her.

She rushed into the bedroom with a dirty smile, already peeling her dress from her body. "Let's get down to business, shall we?"

God, he loved her.

<hr>

"MAYA, SLOW DOWN," Kenny said.

She stopped pushing her dress down her body. "Why? Is there an intruder in the bathroom that you missed?"

"No," Kenny replied as he stripped his jacket off of his body. "But let's go slow."

She rolled her eyes. "We can go slow for round two. Get naked, babe."

He laughed and shook his head – even as he was unbuttoning his shirt. "It's almost Valentine's Day. Don't you want it to be special?"

She stepped out of her dress and put her hands on her hips. She stood there glaring at him in just a very skimpy pair of lace boy shorts and her heels. "I can leave my shoes on if you want. Is that special enough? Also, it's not technically Valentine's Day yet. We've still got a few hours. Oh," she squealed, "but I can give you one of your Valentine's presents now."

"*One* of my presents?" he asked with a soft smile. "You got me a present? You got me more than one present?"

His eyes were wide with surprise and the corners of his mouth were lifting into a smile. It was such an innocent look and it made her heart swell.

"Of course I did, babe," she whispered. She turned to the closet and bent to push open her suitcase. She heard Kenny groan behind her. She smiled as she rooted round in her suitcase, pushing aside her regular mesh bag of lingerie for the second mesh bag. Inside she found the slightly bigger wrapped gift box. She turned around with a triumphant grin on her face. "I wrapped it myself."

He sat on the foot of the bed and watched her as she walked the present over to him. "It looks professionally wrapped," he said.

She bounced onto the bed next to him and placed the gift in his hands. "I had winter jobs at Macy's from like sixteen until I went to business school. I've still got it."

He turned to her and smiled. "Thank you."

"What are you thanking me for? You haven't even opened it yet. Come on."

Kenny opened the gift carefully and reverently. It was adorable.

Maya had begun preparing for Valentine's Day just after the new year. She'd made a list of presents he might like in the back of the notebook where she recorded all of her work stats, scribbling options that she could research in her downtime. She'd narrowed it down to three things in a heartbeat. She'd spent days wrapping them perfectly and figuring out how to give them to him. She'd had to adjust her plans a little now that they were in Hong Kong and not... doing whatever he had planned beforehand. She'd wanted to be wearing the black lace outfit for this gift. But in the end it didn't really matter what she was wearing. Just that she got to see his face as he opened it. Besides, naked from the waist up in killer heels was as good an outfit as any.

When it was unwrapped, he turned to her. His face was beet red. "I really should have expected this."

"You really should have," Maya said, tapping the box with her index finger. "Your wish is my command. Wanna try it out now?" she whispered against his jaw.

He smiled shyly, but she could tell as the blush spread over his cheeks that he was excited. "Will you be gentle with me?"

She closed her eyes and sighed softly. "God you're wonderful," she moaned. She tilted her head and he brushed his mouth to hers. "We'll go slow," she promised.

He slipped his tongue into her mouth. That answer was perfectly fine by her.

▭

MAYA WAS a woman of her word. She was also even more gentle than he'd expected. Just one more thing for Kenny to love about her.

She took his hand and walked him to the bathroom. They stood at the bathroom sink and opened the box. She pulled the cock ring out and they washed it together as Maya talked him through his options for how to wear it. While they waited for it to dry, Maya undressed Kenny and let him unbuckle her heels and pull her panties down her legs. She laid him down and dashed back into the bathroom. She smiled at him and winked when she returned, a handful of condoms in one hand and a small bottle of lube in the other. The cock ring dangling from her left ring finger. He dissolved into loud peals of laughter.

Maya crawled onto the bed next to him. "Alright, you stay still while I work, mister."

Kenny opened his eyes to see that she was talking to his dick. He laughed louder. But he choked on his giggles when her hand touched his cock. His muscles tensed.

"Shhh," she cooed to his penis.

The absurdity of the situation helped him relax. "Why are you shushing my dick? It doesn't speak." His jaw tightened as she rolled a condom down his shaft, trying – praying – not to get hard.

"Don't knock my methods," Maya said and gently rubbed some of the lube over his shaft. "Tell me if I hurt you."

He felt the ring descend onto his shaft. He grunted as she

maneuvered one ball through it and then the other. One of his legs twitched and he only remembered to breathe when she put a hand on his stomach, stroking the soft hair below his belly button gently.

"Are you okay?"

"It's… It feels… different."

"Is it too tight? I can take it off."

He shook his head. "No, it's okay. I'm-" he took a deep breath. "Just let me adjust."

She laid down on the bed next to him on her side, pressing herself into his body. She brushed her leg onto his. "Take all the time you need," she said and placed a kiss on his chest.

Kenny moved his arm to wrap around her shoulders and rub his hand up and down her back. She shivered against him and kissed his chest again.

"How many presents did you get me?" he asked, once his breath returned to normal.

She lifted her torso and turned to him, "Three."

"Are you going to give me another one tonight?"

She smiled, "Well, I am going to let you have sex with me. That is a gift."

He smiled. "I'll take that as a no."

"How do you feel?" she whispered.

"Better."

"Do you want to wait some more? Or are you ready for the next step?"

He squinted at her, "What's the next step?"

"I want to sit on your face."

"Next step," he said quickly.

She laughed. "We don't have to rush."

"We're not rushing. I'm ready. Let's go. Hop on."

She fell onto her back and laughed.

He turned to cover her, nuzzling her neck. "Come on. I'm ready. I promise," he whispered, as he kissed her cheek.

Maya turned to him. "Don't just say that because you're

horny. I said I would be gentle." She cupped his cheek. "I don't want to hurt you."

He lifted an eyebrow and looked down his body.

Maya smiled at his dick, semi-hard and hardening. But she wiped the smile off her face and turned to him. "Does it hurt? Be honest."

Kenny shook his head. "It definitely feels weird. But no, it doesn't hurt."

Her eyes darted back to his dick. It twitched and she smiled. "You have to promise to tell me if you feel hurt or numb or anything," she said.

He settled back on the bed and smiled, "Promise."

She sat up on her knees. He smiled up at her. She leaned over his head and licked his lips. "Say it again."

"Hop on," he said, because he knew exactly what she wanted to hear. They laughed together as she crawled up to the head of the bed. His hands grabbed at her thighs and moved around her body to squeeze her ass. She moaned.

"Come here, baby," he whispered against her sex as she lowered onto his mouth.

He licked up and down her lips, first softly, tentatively, tasting her in short swipes of his tongue. Maya sighed and melted into his touch. He smiled against her pussy and increased the pressure, flattening his tongue against her sex. Swiping between her folds. Teasing her entrance.

He felt his dick twitch as it grew. It felt different, harder, more intense. He tightened his arms around her waist and pulled her down onto his face.

"Oh my god," she gasped and slapped two hands onto his chest, grinding her sex down onto his mouth. She tightened her thighs around his head. He laughed as he ate her like a starving man, licking and sucking at her and settling his chin against her clit.

She groaned and began to ride his face, grinding her pussy

against his mouth. This was his favorite part. He opened his mouth and stuck out his tongue, moving his hands to her ass, encouraging her to take every bit of pleasure from him. She was close. He could feel it. Her thighs were shaking and her soft gasps had turned into insistent moans. He was so focused on her that his hips spasmed off the bed when her hand closed over the head of his dick. The shock was so great that he bucked Maya off of him.

Maya yelped and collapsed onto the bed, laughing hysterically.

"Holy fuck, what was that?" he yelled.

"I told you you'd be really sensitive," Maya said around her laughter.

"How sensitive?" he asked in a soft, lustful whisper.

She stopped laughing and looked at him with a smile. "You think you're ready to find out?"

He chuckled and shook his head. "Not at all."

That answer made her happy and she sat up on her knees. She pushed him back down. "Alright, remember you asked for this."

He sucked in a breath as she moved down the bed and straddled his lap. He was panting and clutching at the sheets as she sank ever so slowly onto his length. "Oh my god," it was his turn to breathe.

"Tell me about it," she replied in a kind of strained moan. "You always feel great, but… oh my god."

"Yeah," he gasped. "I know that feeling."

"You ready?" she asked.

He shook his head then switched to nod quickly.

She laughed.

He groaned as her pussy clenched and then unclenched around him rhythmically.

She sat back on her heels and then reached for his hands. "Here, babe. Hold onto me." She settled his hands onto her hips. She put her hands on his chest. They made eye contact and she waited until he could nod – and only nod – that he was ready.

Having sex with Maya had never been boring or just alright. Every time Kenny had the pleasure of touching and tasting and fucking her was like a religious experience as far as he was concerned. But *this*. This was something else.

Maya rotated her hips and ground into him in such an achingly slow pace that it was just on the edge of painful. He practically begged her to speed up. "Please," he gasped. "It's… fuck, it's too much." His fingers dug into her flesh, trying to spur her along.

She gave him a wicked smile as she sat back and moved against him faster and then faster.

He kept his eyes on her as she lifted her breasts to lick and suck at her nipples as she met his gaze.

"Oh god," he groaned. "I feel like I'm going to burst."

She laughed as he flipped her onto her back.

He maybe wanted to go slow. He maybe wanted to take his time and feed her his dick in long strokes so that she could become a babbling mess right along with him. But he could hardly control himself. He sat back on his knees, grabbed her waist and plowed into her rough and deep, until Maya's nails were scraping at his chest.

He licked his thumb and began to stroke her clit. She came immediately. The vibrations of her sex made his body shudder. He crumpled on top of her, his own intense arousal and need to come the only things keeping his hips moving. She wrapped her arms around him as he fucked her deep and groaned "fuckfuckfuck" into her ear as she came again.

Sometimes Maya's orgasms triggered his own. Sometimes he had to grit his teeth and force himself to last long enough for her to come. But he had never been so hard or so aroused. He lifted onto his hands to look down at her. Some sweat from his forehead dripped onto her cheek. She moved one hand onto his forehead to wipe away the moisture and then behind his neck to pull him down. She wrapped the other arm around his back. It took some maneuvering to get her hand over his ass and just below his ball sack. Just a soft press of her fingers onto his perineum and he came – his hips still pounding into her – in a forceful gush that made his breath hitch and bright pops of light flash behind his eyelids. His body was wracked with violent shudders as he called out her name.

Kenny collapsed onto Maya – his body twitching and shuddering like never before. She wrapped her legs and arms around him, holding him close, kissing his face gently and murmuring soothing words. Kenny wasn't sure how long it took for his wheezing breaths and pounding heartbeat to return to normal, or for the quakes to subside, but when they did Maya rolled him onto his back. She kissed him one more time and then gently – so gently, just like she'd promised – slipped his dick from the cock ring and the condom.

"A mess," she teased.

He was too exhausted to laugh, but his abs jumped as he tried. She went to the bathroom and he heard the water running. He must have fallen asleep because the next thing he knew she was crawling into bed next to him and arranging the flat sheet over their bodies.

She wrapped her body around his side and kissed his chest gently before resting her head over his heart.

"I love you," he said. And then fell asleep.

seven

Maya was lying on the bed, facing Kenny. Waiting. Staring at the side of his face intently. He didn't snore so the only way she could tell if he was asleep or awake was by the slow rise and fall of his chest. She put her hand over his heart. He shifted and she quickly closed her eyes.

She waited a few seconds before peeking one eye open. He was still asleep. She sighed.

"Are you waiting for me to wake up?" Kenny mumbled.

Maya shot up onto her elbow and looked down at his still closed eyes. "How long have you been awake?"

He reached out for her left leg and pulled it and her half on top of him, his eyes still closed. "A few minutes," he said as his hands coasted over her bare thigh. "How long have you been watching me sleep?"

She shivered. She loved his first thing in the morning voice, deep and raspy and intimate. "A few minutes more."

He smiled. "Liar." He turned his head to finally open his eyes. "Happy Valentine's Day," he rasped.

Her sex clenched her and she smiled down at him sweetly. "Happy Valentine's Day." She could feel the blush spreading over her entire body. "You ready for your next present?"

He shook his head and laughed. "No. After last night, absolutely not. I have never in my life come that hard."

Maya sat fully up and felt a kind of power she'd never have imagined. "So I put it on you so good-"

"Not good. Way past good," he interjected.

"That I've got you running scared?"

He grabbed her and pulled her fully on top of him. She straddled his lap and her bare sex pressed into his briefly. They both moaned. "Sorry," he whispered. "I didn't realize you were bare." He gulped. "And wet."

Maya could have smiled. Kenny was like vitamins for her self-esteem, which was already very very healthy. She couldn't imagine her life without him. "I'm always wet for you," she said, easing off of his hardening dick. "But if you need a break, I'm a benevolent mistress. Oh," she perked up. "Don't let me forget that. I have an idea for a series we can do on my channel."

"Maya," Kenny mumbled and pulled her down to him with a laugh.

She laid on top of him, enjoying the way his hard body felt under hers. And his arms around her, kneading her flesh and pulling her close. "Come on. Give it to me."

Maya gently cupped his face. "Please be more specific," she purred.

"I'm ready for my second present."

She smiled. "Okay, close your eyes." He did.

She took a second to appreciate him. His long dark eyelashes, the lingering blush on his cheeks, his perfect mouth, the tip of his nose, the sparse, dark stubble on his jaw. Technically Maya had spent weeks thinking about what to give Kenny for their first Valentine's Day together. But this gift had taken no time at all to consider. It was the most natural. She dipped her head and kissed his chin and the corner of his mouth and then the rise of his cheek. "I love you, too."

His eyes flew open and he nearly threw her off of him as he sat up.

It wasn't the response she was expecting. Especially not after last night. She crawled off him and sat, with her legs off to one side. He rubbed his eyes and looked at her. "Can you say that again please?"

Maya fisted her hands in the sheets beneath her. "It's a little early. I've been with people longer and never even *thought* of saying it. And I had planned it out better than this. I thought, you know, a little morning sex. Maybe room service just in case we weren't at my apartment. I also bought this piece of lingerie that I knew would make you tongue-tied."

"Maya," Kenny said, grabbing her hands and pulling them to his chest. "Please just say it again."

"I love you," she whispered and then rushed on. "Last night you said you loved me so I thought I should say I love you, too."

He pulled her back onto his lap and kissed her jaw and her mouth and she laughed in excitement. "One more time."

She cupped the back of his head and held him still while she lowered her mouth to his. "I love you," she whispered again.

He wrapped his arms around her and held her close. It wasn't at all how she'd planned. She didn't wake up early to wash her face and brush her teeth and do her hair and makeup. And they fumbled a bit trying to grab a condom from the nightstand and get it on without having to let each other go. They laughed and mumbled around kisses. And gasped and groaned as she settled onto his dick. It was comfortable and imperfect and warm and gentle and exactly what Maya had wanted from the person who made her forget every shitty, lonely Valentine's Day she'd had before him.

"HOW DO I LOOK?" he asked.

She motioned for him to turn around and she leaned back on her hands to watch. His blue suit and cream shirt fit him perfectly. They'd only been dating a few months but in their time together she'd come to enjoy how different Kenny could look day-to-day. Sometimes he went to work in a nice gray or black suit and came home in a completely different outfit like a nice pair of jeans, or basketball shorts and a hoodie or even, one time, a pair of dark blue coveralls stained with grease. All the many outfits had proven to Maya was that she liked him in whatever he was wearing. She liked him a lot. And then she remembered that she didn't have to temper her own feelings. Not even to herself. She loved him. And he loved her.

She made eye contact with him and sucked her bottom lip into her mouth, "Like a wealthy do-gooder who had the best sex of his life last night."

He snorted, "Sounds more than right. What are you getting up to today?"

"I was thinking I'd hang out by the pool and drink something fruity," she said.

He walked to her and kissed her on the tip of her nose. "Good."

"Unless…" she started to say, but was interrupted by a knocking on the suite's door.

Maya knew intellectually that Kenny was a spy, but it was so hard to imagine him as anything other than the smiling, blushing, laughing man that she loved. It was only in those moments where she saw the other side of him that she was reminded that the smiling, blushing, laughing man that she loved was also highly trained and dangerous. At the sound of the knock on the door, his formerly relaxed, well-fucked posture turned rigid and expectant. He grabbed his phone from the bedside table and headed toward the sitting room.

Maya tiptoed toward the bedroom door and just peeked around it to watch Kenny. First he moved to a case on the coffee table and grabbed a small black gun from inside it. He shut his laptop closed and tipped the suitcase with all of his tech inside closed with his left foot as he passed. All the while, his eyes were on the door. "Who is it?"

"I have an invitation from Prince Mohammed, sir." Someone called from the other side of the door.

Maya angled herself further behind the bedroom door. Staying out of sight.

Kenny moved the gun behind his back and opened the door with his free hand.

Maya couldn't hear their conversation. She waited with bated breath.

"Thank you," Kenny said and closed the door. He walked backwards from the door.

"Can I come out now?" Maya whispered.

He turned to her and nodded.

She rushed into the sitting room. "What's up?"

Kenny placed his gun back into its case and then handed the envelope in his hand over to her. "Change of plans," he said. "You're going to need another dress."

The card stock in Maya's hands was thick. "Closing event," she read.

Kenny hooked one of his index fingers into the belt of her robe, undoing it and then pulling the robe apart. He gently cupped her breasts.

"So how fancy are we talking?" she asked as his hands wandered over her body.

He chuckled and brushed his mouth over her collarbone. "Does it matter? You could wear nothing and be the best dressed person in the room." He stilled and lifted his head to make eye contact with her. "But you should wear clothes."

She chuckled. "Thanks for clarifying. I only brought the one dress. Looks like I'm going to have to go shopping. And it's probably going to be expensive and imported. That's assuming I can even find anything in my size," she said.

He kissed her shoulder one more time before walking to the desk on the other side of the room. He opened his cover wallet and pulled a credit card from it. "Spend as much as you need to," he said as he handed the card over.

She cocked one eyebrow up at him. "Did you… think I wasn't?"

He laughed and wrapped his arms around her waist under her robe. She threw her arms around his shoulders. "Can I put in a request for something low cut? Maybe with a slit?" he asked.

"I'll do my best," she giggled. "So… about your Valentine's Day plans?"

He frowned. "I'm really sorry we couldn't do the thing I'd planned for us."

"Which was?"

He shook his head and kissed her chin, "I'm still not telling you."

"Why not?"

"Just because we're not doing it today doesn't mean we won't do it tomorrow or the day after that or next Valentine's Day," he whispered.

She smiled softly at him, feeling her cheeks warm as he smiled back.

"But don't worry. I still have your present."

"I like presents," she whispered. "Gimme."

He shook his head and ground his hips against her core, "Not yet. After the party."

"Why? I've literally given you two presents already."

"Three," he corrected. "I've decided that the face-sitting was its own gift."

She grinned, "You're damn right it was."

He laughed and unwrapped his arms from around her. He kissed her chin, and then down her neck. He stooped to lift her breasts, locked eyes with her and then circled his tongue over one and then the other nipple.

She gasped. "If you aren't going to keep going south, you better stop right now."

He smiled up at her wickedly and then kissed her left nipple before releasing her breasts. She frowned. He pecked her on the lips, whispered "later" and then stepped away from her.

"That was evil," she called after him as he turned and headed to the door. "When have I ever left you unsatisfied?"

He laughed but kept moving, snatching up a messenger bag thrown over the desk chair.

"This present better be fucking perfect," she yelled after him.

"Love you too," he yelled back.

Her mouth fell open in a shocked smile. It was going to take her a while to adjust to hearing those words from him. It sounded better than she'd let herself dream.

KENNY WALKED CONFIDENTLY down the hallway, his messenger bag draped across his body. A woman stepped out of her hotel room. He immediately remembered her face from last night's party. He'd seen her speaking to Maya. She and Kenny made eye contact. They smiled politely and he stepped out of her way as they passed each other. He remained alert and listened to her muffled steps behind him as they faded away. He turned to look at her back.

Outside of room 1012, he turned to look down the hall again. The woman was stepping onto the elevator. She didn't turn to look at him as she did. Good.

He knocked twice in rapid succession. Waited three seconds and then knocked once more. The door swung open immediately. He stepped inside. The room was smaller than the one he was sharing with Maya. It was a regular hotel room rather than a suite, with a small cramped sitting area and two chairs huddled around a low coffee table.

In one of the chairs, a man with dark hair and light brown skin was looking at him.

"Do you know Sanchez?" Carlisle asked.

Kenny shook his head, "But I know your reputation. It's nice to meet you."

Sanchez stood and extended his hand to Kenny with an easy smile. "Finally, a field mouse with some manners."

"Field mouse?" Kenny said as he shook Sanchez's hand.

"Just a friendly nickname for you field agents," Sanchez said. "What do you call us?"

Kenny sat in the other chair and shrugged, "Robots."

There was a beat of silence before Sanchez and Carlisle burst into laughter. "I like it," Sanchez said.

"You would. Let's get down to business, shall we?" He turned to Kenny. "Your hacker?"

"Oh yeah." Kenny pulled his cell phone from his pocket. He dialed Chanté's number and put it on speaker. The phone rang twice and then the call disconnected.

"Technical difficulties?" Sanchez asked.

Kenny shook his head as he opened his secure network laptop. He picked up Chanté's call immediately.

"Hey, handsome," she breathed.

"Hey," Kenny said and looked her over. She sounded tired, stressed maybe? Kenny couldn't be sure. It was always so hard to tell with Chanté. Especially when she was far away. When she wanted to hide herself, she always made sure there was at least one body of water between them. "Everything alright?"

"Yep," she said, too quickly. "What's up?"

"We need a debrief," Sanchez said.

Chanté's face lit up. "Great voice. Turn me toward him, Ken Doll."

Carlisle snickered.

"No wonder you weren't offended by field mouse," Sanchez breathed.

Kenny rolled his eyes and turned his laptop so that the other men could see her.

"Chanté, this is Sanchez, the voice, and Carlisle."

"Carlisle," Chanté said. "Kierra didn't tell me you were so… big? How was New Year's Eve in Edinburgh?"

Kenny watched as Carlisle turned bright red. "She told you about that?"

"Can you tell me?" Sanchez asked.

"I actually don't want to know," Kenny butted in.

He stood from his chair and saw the look Chanté was aiming at Carlisle, interested and aroused. But still, something was off. "Don't worry, she doesn't kiss and tell. But I'm nosey and there is definitely something to tell. And I bet it's good."

"It damn sure better be," Sanchez said.

"Chanté, can we get to work?" Kenny asked.

"Please," Carlisle breathed.

She sighed. "Oh okay. So, I monitored Prince Mohammed's bodyguard's movements all yesterday. Nothing out of the ordinary as far as I could see. He was either in the Prince's room, the conference floor or doing security sweeps of the service stairs. I sifted through the info from last night's cocktail hour. Every face scan you gave me checked out. And there was nothing out of the ordinary on the phone we broke into. If the intel we got was real, the threat has to be coming from inside the house so to speak."

"That's what I was afraid of," Kenny breathed. "It could be anyone, a bodyguard, another delegate, one of their bodyguards, the wait staff; literally anyone. And it could happen at any time."

Chanté nodded dispassionately. Which made Kenny very uncomfortable. "Anything else?" he asked.

"Nothing. Hey, I already talked to Monica, but I need to dip out on you guys a little early. I have something else I'm working on. But if you need me quick, Kierra knows how to find me."

Carlisle and Sanchez nodded.

Kenny scooped up his laptop and walked to the other side of the room. "Are you sure everything's alright?"

She smiled sadly at him. "It's fine. *I'm* fine."

"Is this about Asif?"

She bit her lip rather than lie to him.

He exhaled a pained breath. "Chanté-"

"I'm a big girl, Kenny. Just… save the Prince, give Maya your great Valentine's present and I'll see you soon."

"How soon?"

She shook her head. "Not sure yet." She smiled then, "But if I get in trouble, you're the first person I'll call. Always."

"You better," he said.

"Oh, and I'm still working on that thing you gave me. No luck yet."

Kenny exhaled. "Okay thanks."

"No problem. Tell our girl I said hi."

"Will do. You be careful," he said.

She gave him her best smile. She almost looked like herself again. "Yeah, I don't know what that is. Bye, Ken Doll."

"Bye Chanté," he exhaled. She disconnected the video call immediately.

"So is she single?" Sanchez asked from behind him.

Kenny turned and squinted at him. "That's my best friend, dude."

"Aren't you dating Kierra's best friend though?" Carlisle said.

Sanchez and Carlisle bumped fists.

Kenny rolled his eyes. He wished Monica was here in that moment. He would gladly let her take over and get everyone on task. But she wasn't. So the responsibility of getting everyone else back on track was up to him. "I have a plan. Do you want to hear it or get my friend's phone number?"

"I mean, ideally we can do both."

"We can't. So let's get to work."

Sanchez sighed and Carlisle patted him on the shoulder to console him. Kenny rolled his eyes again. Fuck, this was not how he'd wanted to spend his Valentine's Day.

He walked across the room and sank back into his chair. "Okay look. We have to assume that whoever is going to try and kill Prince Mohammed isn't going to do it at night in his suite or something. If so, why even let him come here? Why even let him make it to the final day of the summit? If someone is going to try and take him out and has been here all along, we should assume that they're going to do it at the closing reception."

"Why?" Carlisle asked.

"Maximum spectacle. The delegates have kept the media at bay except for a few journalists and photographers who are on an embargo until tomorrow morning. What if, instead of reporting on the terms of trade and peace treaties, they report on the assassination of the future king of Qatar? That story is going to spread faster and wider than the Summit negotiations ever would. And it'll send a clear message to anyone who might consider trying something like this again."

"Oh, you're good," Sanchez said.

Kenny tried not to let the compliment go to his head. He had a job to do and he wanted to get it done quickly and efficiently to salvage what little of this day for himself and Maya as he could.

"So, what's the plan?" Carlisle asked.

"I made my pitch to the Prince. If he's interested, I'm hoping to stay close to him at the party. If he's not, we'll have to keep our eyes on him and stay as close as possible and hope we can see the assassination before it succeeds."

"Is that a plan?" Sanchez said.

Kenny opened his mouth to answer but Carlisle cut him off. "It's close enough."

He nodded at Kenny and Kenny nodded back.

Kenny wondered if this was how Monica felt. To be trusted by the people who were counting on her to lead them into the fray. Trusting her to get them out safe. If so, he had an entirely new level of respect for her. And he wasn't so certain anymore that he was in a rush to fill her shoes.

MAYA FELT as if she was walking on a carpet of clouds. Were three simple words and a few great orgasms supposed to do that to her? Was this what it was like to be in a healthy relationship? She wasn't entirely sure, but if this was what her life would be like with Kenny, she felt ecstatic. And even more excited to give him his third and final gift.

But that could wait.

Right now, she was walking on clouds through the lobby and it was only when she stepped out of the air-conditioned hotel into the mild, and slightly humid, late morning heat that she realized she didn't have any idea where the hell she was going. And she started laughing. She probably looked hysterical, but she didn't care. She wanted to tell everyone who was looking at her with wary eyes that she fucked her cute boyfriend to sleep last night and told him she loved him this morning and he loved her back. And this was their first Valentine's Day together. And she might have been about to do just that when someone tapped her on the shoulder. She turned around.

"Rita," she exclaimed.

The woman looked taken aback and her smile was confused but kind. "You're in a good mood today."

Maya shook her head, her braids swaying, "Great mood. I'm in a great mood today."

"Ah, it's Valentine's Day."

Maya nodded.

"Well, where is your boyfriend?"

"Oh, he's working. It's okay," Maya said. "We're going to the closing event later and I need to find a dress."

Rita's eyes traveled down Maya's body and back up to her face. "I don't know how to tell you this, but you might have a hard time finding something in your size, beautiful as it is."

Maya smiled, enjoying the compliment. "Don't worry, I have a plan. Kind of. Really, I just need a skirt. Or fabric. I'm resourceful," Maya said. What she didn't say was that she only wanted something easy to get under or off. It was Valentine's Day after all.

Rita smiled, "Then I might be able to help you. I was heading out to do a little shopping myself. Would you like to go together?"

Maya nodded, "I'd love to."

Just as she agreed, a car pulled up next to the curb. Rita nodded for Maya to follow her and they were off.

KENNY, Carlisle and Sanchez had gone over possible take downs and extractions for most of the afternoon. On the way back to his suite, he snuck into the ballroom. Hotel staff were setting up for the event. He kept out of their way and walked around the room, needing to have a concept of its size before it was full of people. Once he was satisfied, he took the elevator to his floor, hoping as he ascended that Maya would be there when he arrived. She wasn't. He sighed and changed into his workout clothes and headed down to the gym. He ran a few miles on a treadmill and used the physical exertion to soothe and order his mind before the party.

He was sweaty and tired and considering a nap when he pushed open the door. His steps faltered at the sight of Maya in a bodysuit he'd never seen before – because he'd seen them all – posing on the couch, looking over her shoulder, directly at him.

The suit was a champagne lace that covered her lower back and, from what he could tell, her breasts and stomach. The lace was rimmed with a matching satin ribbon that caged her back and striped along her sides. The gentle rolls of flesh poked delicately through the large rectangles of space created by the ribbon. The gorgeous rounds of her ass were complete bare. Her beautiful light brown skin seemed to glow against the pale fabric just barely covering her body. He'd felt tired just two seconds ago but the sight of her made his entire body come to life.

"Are you coming in or not? Either way, you maybe want to shut the door," she said, the sound of her suppressed laughter making his balls ache.

"I-" He couldn't quite think what to say but he stepped fully into the room, closing the door behind him. "Is that what you bought when you were out?" He finally spluttered.

"Yeah, right. I could barely find a pair of pants in my size." She climbed off the couch and faced him. His blood was pounding in his ears when he saw the front of the body suit, the intricate lace obscuring her body, but not quite hiding her dark areoles and then disappearing between the cleft of her legs. His eyes focused on that cleft as she walked toward him.

"You brought that with you?" he asked.

"Yep. It was one of the outfits I was going to use to seduce you today."

He swallowed thickly and nodded. "It worked." And then he finally managed to raise his head. "One of?"

She stopped in front of him, not close enough to touch. And he wouldn't. He was slick with sweat from his workout and from staring at her. But fuck if he didn't want her to slide her entire body and that lace and satin all over him.

"I didn't pack for a diplomatic event, so I'm going to have to improvise."

"No. Maya, you can't- you can't wear that to this event. I won't..." he shook his head. "No one will be able to concentrate. Not even the damn assassin."

"Then great, he won't be able to kill your prince."

"Not this time. We need him to try this time. And apparently that's going to mean that you can't wear that," he said with equal parts conviction and sadness.

"Calm down, babe. I wasn't going to show up in *just* this. Although that would be a moment. I found a silky dress to go over this. It's supposed to be loose and flowing, but on me it's tight," she hissed that last word. "Very tight. It won't have a low neckline or slit like you wanted. Well, the dress doesn't have a slit but I-"

"Maya," he groaned.

She giggled, "All the best bits will be covered. I promise. And I'll show you just as soon as you help me."

"Help you do what?"

She turned and walked back to the couch. He actually had to grip his dick and close his eyes and count to five. He was afraid he was going to come in his pants at the way the flesh at her thighs and hips tried to entrance him with every step she took and the soft jiggle of her thighs. It wouldn't have been the first time that had happened.

She crawled back onto the couch and turned to look at him over her shoulder, pushing her long braids to the back and aiming her best sultry glare at him. "What do you think about these pics for next month's VIP viewer perks?"

He squeezed his dick one more time, before he felt strong enough to answer. "If they're anything like me, they'll ask you for a higher tier so they can give you more money once they see it."

"That's what I thought," she nodded. "So come on, help

me get a good shot and I'll help you with my best friend in your pants."

"This is the best Valentine's Day of my life," Kenny breathed before walking across the room to pick up her DSLR.

---

eight

"Keep your eyes forward, sir," Maya said. She watched his mouth curve into a smile in the reflective elevator doors. Her head fell forward and she blushed as his lips grazed her cheek. She felt him smile against her skin. "I spent so much time on this makeup," she whined as he pulled her against him.

"And it's beautiful," he said before licking the seam of her lips. "You taste like cherries."

"I've invested in flavored lip gloss since you kiss all of my lipstick off anyway."

He pressed his mouth to hers, proving her point. "How many flavors?"

She wrapped her arms around his shoulders. "You'll just have to keep kissing me unexpectedly to find out."

"Deal," he said and then walked her to the elevator wall, kissing her, stroking her tongue with his, clutching at her body through the sumptuous slip of fabric cleaving to every inch of her.

In the corner, he pulled back and leveled her with a serious look. "I know this is going to be hard for you, but you need to go as under the radar as possible."

"Babe. You've seen me. You've seen this dress. You've seen

what's *underneath* this dress. Under the radar is not my style. But," she said, before he could launch into his lecture again. "I promise to stay away from the Prince and to keep my eyes on all the exits."

His face was grave. Maya knew that Kenny wanted nothing more than to leave her safe in their hotel suite, but she was part of his cover. And she'd spent a tiny fortune on this glorified nightie. Also, her makeup really was immaculate. So she gave him her softest eyes and held his stare until he relented.

He leaned his forehead against hers. "What's my third gift?" he whispered.

"Uh, excuse me. Where's my first gift? Valentine's Day is almost over."

He smiled and then sucked her bottom lip into his mouth, pulling her into a quiet and emotional kiss. The elevator doors dinged and opened, but Kenny only released her mouth. "I was going to take you to Florida to meet my parents," he said.

Maya's mouth fell open. "What?"

"I wanted them to meet you. I've never felt like this about anyone before. And I wanted the three most important people in my life to know each other just in case…"

Maya's eyes became wet instantly. Kenny moved one hand from her waist to dab at her tears.

"I wanted you to know how important you are to me," he said, not quite finishing the earlier sentence. "That was one of your gifts."

"Oh my god, my makeup," she wailed, tears falling down her face.

The elevator dinged and the doors slid closed.

Kenny took a handkerchief from his suit pocket and stroked her arms as Maya dabbed at her eyes gently.

"You're lucky I used my good powder and setting spray," she said in a still teary voice.

"I don't know what that means, but okay."

"It means you were going to take me to meet your parents and you decided to tell me this now?"

He ducked his head and smiled. "I didn't plan to. It's just… there's so much I don't know about this party and I really don't have time for this. But I don't ever want to leave without you knowing that I love you. That I've been falling in love with you since the first moment I saw you. Don't cry again," he said with a laugh.

"Then stop saying romantic things! Apparently I'm unable to handle this right now."

Kenny cupped her face and tilted it so that he could look into her eyes. "You're my first actual Valentine," he said.

"What?!" she shrieked again.

"I've never actually been in a relationship on Valentine's Day. Relationships were never my priority and apparently girls don't like that."

"Wow, shocker," she laughed and dabbed at the corners of her eyes.

"You're the first person I've ever put before my job or my plans for the future. And you are absolutely worth it. And once I figure out what the fuck is happening at this party, I'm going to show you how important you are for whatever time we have left on our first Valentine's Day. And our next Valentine's Day and for as long as you'll have me." He was smiling at her, eyes alight with happiness. All Maya could do was bite her lips closed.

"Um… Maya," he finally said. "Don't you have anything to say?"

She shook her head. His face fell.

She sighed. "I'm afraid if I talk, I'm going to start crying again." And then she did.

▭

"YOU'RE LATE," Carlisle whispered to him over the rim of a tumbler that Kenny knew would be filled with tonic water.

"It's Valentine's Day," Kenny offered as his only answer.

Carlisle laughed.

"Sanchez?"

"I'm here," the man said, extending a tray toward him with one more glass of champagne atop it.

Kenny took it and brought it to his mouth.

"I thought you were here with a girlfriend?" Sanchez asked.

Carlisle answered for him. "There she is."

They all turned as Maya walked into the room. She looked beautiful and he doubted that anyone could tell that he'd kissed off her lip gloss and she'd cried off some of her makeup. She'd done an excellent job hiding it. She stopped just inside the room to look around and nearly every head turned toward her. She spotted Kenny and began to strut his way.

Kenny wanted to look away. He should look away and locate Prince Mohammed, but he couldn't take his eyes off of her.

"Hello boys," she breathed when she joined them. She took the glass of champagne from Kenny's hand and downed half of it with a wink.

"Hi," Sanchez and Carlisle breathed.

She turned to Kenny and pulled him to her for a kiss. It was not chaste or appropriate for this party. She slipped her tongue into his mouth and sucked on his bottom lip. She moved a hand to swipe her thumb over her lip and then she turned to the other men. "Aren't you all supposed to be saving the world?" she asked before walking away just as quickly as she'd arrived.

They watched her until she disappeared into the crowd. Sanchez turned to Carlisle, "Can I request a transfer to the field mouse division?"

Carlisle squinted, "Don't you have more drinks to serve?"

Sanchez smiled and looked at Kenny. "Put in a good word for me with your boss," he laughed and then walked away.

"You ready?"

"Doesn't really matter. Here come the Prince's bodyguards," Kenny whispered. Carlisle didn't turn to look.

"I'll go get into position," he said. "And I'll keep an eye out for your girl."

Kenny looked at him and said sincerely, "Thank you."

"Mr. Zhang," one of Prince Mohammed's peripheral bodyguards said, just as Carlisle melted into a nearby cluster of people. "Prince Mohammed would like to speak with you."

Kenny nodded and followed one guard as the other fell into step behind him.

Mohammed was sitting at a table by himself, surrounded by bodyguards. He was drinking a cup of tea and out of the corner of his eyes, Kenny watched a waitress bring a selection of hors d'oeuvres straight from the kitchen to his table.

Part of their training at The Academy was to teach new recruits how to process large amounts of information in the field. It was a skill that only got easier with practice. One second he was seriously considering following Maya into the crowd and the next second he was counting the diplomatic and royal guards dotted around the room, noting the almost imperceptible bulge of the firearms in shoulder holsters.

That information dump didn't help him much at the moment, although he knew that it would eventually. But the one piece of information Kenny really wanted – needed – was the identity of whomever had put the hit out on Prince Mohammed and why. Without that, Kenny felt as if he had nothing more than a random selection of puzzle pieces and maybe not even pieces from the same puzzle. But Monica always stressed that there was no point wishing for more information; they had to make use of everything they had and make it work until they got the info they needed. So Kenny focused on doing that.

There were probably three classic ways to assassinate a man under heavy guard: sniper, poisoning and a close-up attack. A sniper was highly unlikely inside the hotel. Kenny noticed one of Mohammed's bodyguards sampling his food. So he moved poisoning down his list.

When Mohammed saw Kenny approaching, he stood from his chair.

"Mr. Zhang," he called with a genuine, if weary smile.

"Prince Mohammed. It's nice to see you again. Congratulations on the successful completion of your Summit."

The Prince smiled warmly. "Please. Have a seat."

Kenny sat and crossed his legs casually.

"I have been thinking about your proposal that I be different, better than your country by investing in my people. This has always been my and my father's plan. This is why the Summit has been so important to us. We want the freedom to live and decide our own futures. I would like to know how *you* can help us do that."

Kenny smiled. "Not every country has your wealth."

The prince nodded.

"Not every country has oil that they can use to negotiate for their own freedom."

The prince nodded again.

Kenny smiled and took a second to compose himself. He realized in that moment that he liked the Prince, which was always a dangerous predicament for someone in his profession. But considering the state of his mission, he decided to lean into it. "I won't lie to you," Kenny began, "I don't have a plan. But when I found out that you were having the Summit I thought 'this is my chance.'"

"Chance?" Mohammed said as his hand tightened around his tea cup.

Kenny ignored the signs of his rising distress, his cover

identity wouldn't have noticed it. Instead he made eye contact with the Prince and smiled wearily. "I know you've had your security look into me. I expect that. It happens everywhere I go because I must sound like a crackpot. I basically spend my free time trying to get rich people and governments to do better. To be better."

"And how successful have you been?"

"Not very," Kenny chuckled. "But when I read what you were trying to do here, I thought there was a chance that you might be my first real success."

"Why do you think you have been so unsuccessful?" he asked and then took a sip of his tea.

"Because rich people like to hoard money and power."

"It is as simple as that?"

"Yes." Out of the corner of his eye, Kenny saw Maya. He would have recognized her skin and the flash of that champagne lace as it peeked through the low back of her dress anywhere.

Prince Mohammed noticed her as well. "You seem distracted."

Kenny knew the Prince was trying to provoke him. It's what he would have done in his position. And in truth it worked for a brief moment. But Kenny took a deep breath and smiled. "All of my work is about breaking down the barriers between people. But I've always been so focused on that, that I haven't made my own connections a priority. Until I met her." He took the opportunity to twist his head to look at Maya.

She was, as usual, the center of a small group of people. But he didn't let his eyes settle on her, even though he wanted to. Instead he found Sanchez in the crowd, circulating amongst the guests. He couldn't locate Carlisle which was either a good sign or a bad sign, as was everything in life. He turned back to the Prince who was watching him.

He took another contemplative sip of his tea. "You do not

have a concrete proposal, but you must have an idea, yes? Why else would you come all the way to Hong Kong to manufacture a meeting with me? I am listening."

Kenny nodded and was just about to begin his spiel – even though he had no idea what to say – when the Prince's bodyguard leaned over his shoulder to whisper to him in Arabic. Kenny pretended that he couldn't understand but he heard as the bodyguard asked him if he would like more tea. Mohammed said that he was fine. The bodyguard nodded and then turned his back to them, as he surveyed the room. There shouldn't have been anything in that movement to catch Kenny's attention. And maybe it wasn't anything in particular. Maybe it was just what his training had always promised; that when you had all the information you needed, all of the puzzle pieces fell into place.

He turned quickly and looked around him to verify the slightly fuzzy feeling in his brain as he put his almost hunch together. Kenny had spent a good portion of his life around firearms and he was very used to them. He was also very used to figuring out who was armed – or more likely to be armed – and who was not. For the past two days he'd been making note of Prince Mohammed's bodyguards who were always armed when he'd seen them. The problem, Kenny realized, was that each of his bodyguards only had one firearm visible in a shoulder holster.

Sure, there was a very good chance that someone had an ankle holster or a knife or literally any number of concealed weapons. And it was entirely possible that the shoulder holsters were visible as a deterrent. It was possible. Reasonable. And yet, when he spotted the slightest disturbance of a gun at this bodyguard's back when he turned around, some things slowly fell into place.

Prince Mohammed had the best security in the world. Of course he did, he had all the money in the world to buy not just security but loyalty. This was why Kenny had always assumed that whoever was after Mohammed had to be a stranger. But if Chanté was right – and Chanté was always right – and there was no one here who *shouldn't* be here, how was someone supposed to get close enough to kill the Prince?

And this bodyguard was the one that Kenny had tagged with the tracker. He hadn't thought of it when Chanté had reported back to him, but why would one of Prince Mohammed's principle bodyguards be doing a security check in the service stairwells? And if there was only one more classic method of assassination left – a close-up attack – who better to enact it than a security guard who was the last line of defense?

He could almost hear Monica's voice in his head, *"The simplest answer is often the right one. Criminals are stupid. People are lazy."*

The simplest answer was obvious. Just as the thought solidified in his mind, there was a disturbance elsewhere in the room. A tray crashed to the floor and someone yelled. The bodyguard turned and grabbed the Prince roughly by the upper arm. He steered him toward a door at the back of the room that Kenny knew led to the service stairs and elevator. From there the Prince and his bodyguard could be at his penthouse in mere minutes. But maybe more importantly, if his bodyguard killed him in the service area, he could be halfway to the airport before anyone even knew the Prince was missing.

The disturbance in the room seemed to have escalated. Kenny heard some yelling, another tray fell, but he had to tune it out, right alongside with his fear for Maya. She was smart. She was wonderful. Carlisle was watching out for her.

Kenny could follow them, but he was unarmed. So he had no choice but to grab the Prince's other arm and yank him out of his bodyguard's grasp.

"What are you doing?" The prince spat in Arabic.

"My apologies, Your Highness. But I think your body-guard is trying to kill you," Kenny replied in Arabic.

Prince Mohammed's face registered shock.

Kenny didn't respond. The bodyguard had reached for his gun. But not the gun in his shoulder holster. He reached for the gun at his back and Kenny understood why. It was small but packed a punch. It would get the job done and be easy to dispose of. But it seemed too small for his large hands. Or at least that's what Kenny thought briefly as he searched for something – anything – to use for a weapon.

The bodyguard aimed his gun at Kenny. "Please move."

"Samir," Prince Mohammed interrupted. "I think there has been a mistake."

A glass crashed onto the floor at Kenny and Samir's feet.

They all turned in the direction the glass had come from. Maya was glaring at Samir.

"Maya, get down," Kenny hissed across the room.

"He's aiming a gun at you," she yelled back. She yelped and ducked under the table in front of her. Kenny turned to see that Samir had turned his gun in her direction.

Kenny was trained to keep cool under pressure. But all of the blood in his body seemed to kick into overdrive at the sight of a gun aimed at Maya. He rushed Samir, grabbing the wrist of his left hand and pushing it up toward the ceiling. Away from Maya. Anywhere but aimed at Maya.

A shot rang out as the gun fired toward the ceiling. Kenny head-butted Samir in the side of the head and kneed him in the side. And then he slammed his hand into Samir's shoulder with the full weight of his body. The man cried out, he fell to his knees and the gun finally fell from his hand.

"Please," Samir whimpered. "Please don't kill me. I had no choice. I did not want to."

Kenny ignored him and looked up, "Sanchez. Carlisle. Cuffs."

He felt Samir exhale. "Alhamdulillah," he breathed.

Sanchez stepped out of the melee of the crowd as guards tried to rush the diplomats to safety. He looked flustered. Annoyed. But there were cuffs in his hand.

Kenny lifted Samir to his feet and turned him around, pulling his arms behind him. Sanchez was almost to him when another shot rang out. Samir went limp in Kenny's arms. Prince Mohammed screamed in anguish behind him.

Kenny turned toward the direction of the gunfire. In the same direction that Maya's glass had come from. He saw her first, her head peeking above a table, her mouth open as she looked up at a woman next to her. By the time Kenny turned in the direction of Maya's gaze, all he saw was a flash of a red dress, dark brown skin and a gun. As he was watching, Carlisle sped from the crowd after the woman. Kenny saw Sanchez kneeling to check Samir's pulse. He looked at Kenny and shook his head. The prince's other guards lifted him from Samir's lifeless body, spiriting him away.

Kenny thought he should go after him. That was the mission. But he knew instinctively that Samir had been working alone. The woman in the red dress was insurance that he either completed the mission or died before he could reveal who had convinced him to do it. Maybe she was always meant to take him out. But he didn't have time to work through that. All that mattered in this moment was getting across the room to Maya.

She was shivering in shock when he got to her. He lifted her and pulled her body to his. "Are you okay?" he whispered into her hair.

"I knew her," she said in a shocked voice.

"What?"

MAYA DIDN'T KNOW what to expect from this party. Was it even really a party? She certainly hadn't expected to start the evening in the bathroom just outside of the ballroom, trying to smush and smudge her makeup around her face to hide tear tracks. But they were happy tear tracks, so it was okay. She decided that slightly mussed makeup aside, she still looked great. And the bathroom mirror agreed. Just outside of the ballroom, guests were queueing through security. Maya took an immense amount of enjoyment at the security guards' red faces and averted eyes as they waved the wand over her body, certainly much faster than was probably wise. If Kenny had needed her to smuggle anything into this event, she felt certain the she could have done it. She made a mental note on the pro column for this dress and bodysuit: it could bring Kenny to his knees *and* would be useful in a mission. It was already worth the money she'd spent on it as far as she was concerned.

She found Kenny and his little friends quickly. Now that she knew what to look for, she could definitely tell they were spies… of a sort. She didn't want to get in the way of their mission and there were hors d'oeuvres to eat. So she flirted with him a bit, drank his champagne – since he would only let it go to waste anyway – and headed for the tray of fruit on the buffet table.

"That dress looks wonderful on you."

She turned with a smile for Rita. "I have you to thank. Without you I probably never would have gone into that shop."

"No thanks necessary. Like I said, it looks as if it was made for you. But who cares about the dress when that bodysuit is making everyone in this party drool into their very expensive wine?"

Maya blushed.

"I hope your boyfriend was just as taken with it?"

"He was a mess," Maya said, remembering how Kenny had pulled her into the shower to fuck her slowly against the tiled wall, whispering how beautiful she was and how much he loved her over and over again.

"Seems as if he wasn't the only one," Rita said with a wink.

Rita followed Maya to an empty table. It was across the room but Maya had a good line of sight to Kenny. If he turned to his left, he would see her and be comforted. The table was empty when they sat but soon enough, emissaries from Libya and Nigeria and an engineer who couldn't manage to raise his eyes above Maya's collarbone through the entire conversation joined them. Maya tried to ignore everyone else and focus on Rita and the waitress and waiter who kept bringing her a choice selection of the best food coming straight from the kitchen. She also pretended that she didn't notice one of Kenny's friends hovering nearby.

It should have been strange, but Maya was having a good time.

"So do you love him?" Rita asked.

Maya popped a piece of sushi into her mouth and nodded. She was barely clothed, but she felt hot. She hadn't even admitted to Kierra or Kaya or Jerome how she felt. If she was getting hot and bothered admitting it to a stranger, she could hardly imagine what she would feel like telling everyone else she loved. But she decided to be thankful that Rita gave her time to practice.

"A lot," she whispered. "I've never been in love with anyone before, but I love him," she said, relishing the words. "So much."

Rita smiled at her and reached out to cover one of Maya's hands. "Hold on to this feeling. Never forget what this feels like."

Maya's smile faltered. In that moment Rita looked so sad. She had seen glimpses of it in their other conversations, but tonight she looked as if the entire weight of the world was on her shoulders. "Who were they?" she asked.

Rita squeezed Maya's hand. "He was someone I can't ever get back."

It wasn't a full answer. It was actually barely an answer. But Maya got a full story in those words and the tone of Rita's voice and her sad eyes. She covered Rita's hand with her own and squeezed reassuringly.

A tray crashed to the floor.

Maya leaned to her left to see around Rita. She saw one of the other spies involved in an altercation with a man in a tuxedo. She frowned and turned to look for Kenny.

She knew what he would want her to do. He would want her to hide or maybe even run out of here and barricade herself in their hotel room. But she couldn't do that. She couldn't leave him. She stood from the table as the diplomats were ushered away to safety or wherever. She honestly didn't care. She wanted to get to Kenny. She saw him across the room, pulling the Prince away from his bodyguard.

"Maya, please get down," Rita said as she crawled calmly from her seat onto the floor.

"No, I can't," she said and then gasped as the bodyguard pulled his gun out and aimed it directly at Kenny. She looked around the room frantic. One of Kenny's friends was still arguing with a man in a tuxedo and the other was fighting with the Prince's other bodyguards, keeping them from advancing on Kenny. Kenny, who was unarmed and momentarily without any backup. Except for her.

Maya's heart was pounding against her chest and she did the first thing that came to mind. She grabbed an empty glass on the table and threw it toward them. It sailed mostly across the distance and then fell to the carpeted floor and rolled the rest of the way.

Kenny and the bodyguard turned toward her with confused eyes. She glared at the bodyguard, communicating with her eyes that she would kill him with her bare hands if he hurt Kenny.

"Maya, get down," Kenny hissed at her.

"He's aiming a gun at you," she yelled. She was just about

to point out that he should have used her distraction to get to safety, but then the bodyguard turned his gun on her and she squeaked and crouched behind the table.

"That was foolish," Rita said.

"I don't care," Maya shot back, her body shaking with rage and fear.

She jumped and cried out when a shot rang out. Tears formed in her eyes and she peeked her head over the table to see. She cried harder with relief as she watched Kenny take the bodyguard down.

"Sanchez. Carlisle. Cuffs," he called out. She had never been so happy to hear his voice.

"Maya," Rita said.

Maya turned to her, swiping at her wet eyes. She looked… normal. And that's when Maya knew that something was wrong.

"I've really enjoyed spending time with you, Maya," Rita said. "It's been a long time since I've enjoyed someone's company."

"Rita?" Maya said completely unsure of what else she should say in this moment.

Rita reached out and grabbed Maya's shoulders and squeezed gently. "You be careful. Love can make you do very stupid things," she whispered. Which, Maya believed, was great advice.

Great advice that seemed incredibly mundane as Rita stood from behind the table, grabbed her purse from atop it and pulled a very large gun from inside. Maya's mouth fell open as she watched Rita aim and take her shot in a span of time that felt like hours and mere seconds. Her head whipped around, Kenny's name on her tongue. She watched as the bodyguard slumped to the floor. She whipped her head back to Rita who turned, winked and then sped away.

Maya stared at the place where Rita had been for however long it took Kenny to get to her. It seemed strange to feel so safe in his arms, after all that had just happened. And yet, *"Love can make you do very stupid things."*

"Are you okay?" he whispered into her hair.

"I knew her," she said, but that wasn't quite the truth.

She clearly hadn't known Rita at all.

nine

"Prince Mohammed's Oil Summit has ended in a shocking failed assassination attempt," the news anchor reported.

Kenny turned off the television, still not ready to hear the news from someone who had no idea what happened. But to be fair, *he* didn't even know what had happened. Sanchez had ushered him and Maya out of the ballroom and waited as a sentinel while they'd quickly packed their belongings. He'd escorted them to the airport and waited until their jet was taxiing away before he left to meet up with Carlisle. Kenny didn't know where Carlisle had gone, but it was safe to assume that he hadn't caught the woman in the red dress. He'd worried about that during the entire flight home, which was quieter and more contemplative than their flight to Hong Kong had been.

The only thing he knew for sure was that the Prince had made it safely back to Doha when the king released a statement on his son's safe return and a rebuke of the "Western countries drunk on their own power, they will stop at nothing to rule the rest of the world." But by that point he and Maya were safe in her apartment in New Jersey and he couldn't make himself care so much about Prince Mohammed. All that mattered was that Maya was safe.

But tomorrow he would have to face Monica and Lane and explain to them what had gone wrong. Kenny hated failing. And even though Mohammed was still alive, somehow he had failed. And it was eating him up. He stood from the couch and walked across the room to the window next to the television. Their street was quiet. Deserted. But it didn't make him feel safe. Knowing that Maya had spent an entire afternoon with an assassin none of them had even known existed was tying a knot in his chest.

He gripped the box in his sweatpants pocket.

He started at the sound of Maya's shower turning on. He wanted desperately to rewind time and go back to a few days before Valentine's Day. He wished he had ignored his phone and let her join him in the shower. He wished he had stuck to his original plans. He wondered again how long he could do this.

"Ahem," Maya said behind him.

Kenny started, clearly lost in his thoughts, he hadn't even heard her shower stop.

When he turned around, his eyes widened and his mouth fell open.

Maya was standing in the hallway, very little of her body covered in the laciest pair of black string panties that did literally nothing to hide her lips and a matching top that somehow covered her sternum and breasts without covering them at all. Her nipples were hard. His mouth was dry.

She put her hands on her hips and smirked at him. "Good morning."

He nodded in response as his eyes roamed up and down her body.

"Are you ready for your last Valentine's Day gift?"

His eyes lifted to hers and he smiled. "Is this it?"

She shook her head. "This is the other outfit I was going to seduce you with."

He wasn't ready to think about Hong Kong yet. Not at all. But this was a worthy exception. "It would have worked. It's working."

Maya snorted in laughter and walked toward him. "Not to be rude, but you could be seduced by me in a paper sack. The lace is just 'cause I like that slack-jawed thing you do."

He nodded again, not entirely comprehending what she was saying because every step revealed a new part of her body behind the lace.

"Come sit here, babe," she said patting the couch next to her.

He was already heading toward her. When he sat next to her on the couch, he reached out and ran his hand over her stomach. She leaned back to give him more access and he was happy to oblige. He could feel her eyes on him as his hands roamed over her body. He played with the tiny straps of her underwear, teased the raw edges of the lace at the creases of her hips. Grabbed her stomach and squeezed. She moaned. His hands moved to cup her breasts. She held her breath until he pulled it from her, pinching her nipples gently and twisting firmly. She whined softly and the sound filled the room.

"We missed the last of our Valentine's Day," she breathed.

He sighed and soothed her nipples with his thumbs. He nodded again.

"Look at me, babe."

It took a few seconds before he dropped his hands to her waist and raised his eyes to hers.

"It's not your fault," she whispered. She leaned forward, cupped the back of his head and pulled his mouth to hers and kissed him softly. "Prince Mohammed is still alive. You completed the mission."

"But I literally put you in danger," he said and pushed away.

"Give me some credit. I stumbled into danger all on my own," she said with a sad smile.

"I'm sorry," he whispered.

"For what? Did you befriend me for some unknown reason? Did you point a gun at me? No," she said before he could "But still…" her. "You didn't do anything but give me a spa day, a few great orgasms, make me happy cry and try to protect me. All while keeping an oil prince from a country I've never heard of alive. You are literally the kind of man I used to dream about." She crawled onto his lap and pushed his shoulders back. "You are the man of my dreams. Now here. Take your last gift even though it's not Valentine's Day anymore," she said, thrusting a small box at him.

She settled back onto his lap and watched him untie the string and pull back the brown wrapping. He opened the box and frowned down at the object inside. He plucked the key and lifted it, turning it around as if there would be some explanation of what it was etched into it. "I don't get it."

"It's a key to my apartment," she replied, gesturing around them.

"I already have a key to your apartment."

"No, you have my spare key. *This* is Kierra's old key. I'm asking you to officially move in with me."

His face lit up. "That's why you haven't found a new roommate?"

She blushed and nodded. "I really did try and find someone. I had a few interviews lined up in the fall and then we were in Hawai'i for so long that my top two choices found other places. I kept accepting applications but every time I thought about someone else moving in, all I could think about was what that would do to our relationship. What if they had questions about you coming and going at literally all hours of the night? What if they freaked out about my webcasts or how loud we get during sex?"

"We?"

"You were literally screaming when we used that cock ring. Don't act brand new," she interjected with a roll of her eyes. "Anyway, I just kept coming up with excuse after excuse for why this or that person wouldn't be a good fit before I finally I realized that I only wanted to live with you. I mean we're basically living together already. When was the last time you even slept down the hall?" she asked, suddenly too shy to look him in the eyes.

"No idea," he said in a hoarse voice. And then he dropped her key back into the box and maneuvered around to pull a small box from his pocket. He held it out on his open palm for her and her face lit up. "Do you want your present now?"

"Oh my god," she squealed, bouncing on his lap. "I didn't want to say anything but I was kind of afraid that you hadn't really gotten me anything."

He shook his head at her and watched as she tore the wrapping paper apart. She opened the box and frowned down at it. "Wait. What's happening?" she said, lifting a key from her own box. "Is this a key to your apartment?"

He shook his head. "That key doesn't go to any lock actually."

She squinted down at him. "Sorry, what now?"

He laughed and moved his left hand to cup the side of her neck, his thumb caressing the curve of her chin. "My parents moved every three or four years for most of my childhood. I was always the new kid, the new Asian kid. Sometimes we lived on base, sometimes we lived in military housing off base. We couldn't paint or really decorate or anything like that. The closest I came to having a home in the way other kids meant it was when I was shuffled off to my grandparents. My room was half of my grandmother's craft room. It was cozy, but it wasn't really mine.

And then I lived in the dorms in college and now," his voice trailed off. Maya's vision blurred as tears filled her eyes. "Before you, I didn't own anything more than I could pack in a duffel and take wherever I needed to go. I live in the apartment down the hall from you but it's just another safe house. Just a pit stop to wherever I'm going. This apartment is closer to my home than anywhere I've lived in years."

Maya swiped at her eyes and pressed her face into his hand.

"The key that I gave you doesn't go anywhere yet because I'm asking if you want to make a home with me. *Create* a home with me," Kenny whispered, tears streaming from his own eyes.

This wasn't the Valentine's Day that Kenny had planned. Technically it wasn't even Valentine's Day anymore. And yet this was what he had hoped for. Maya in his arms, kissing him, the salt of their tears adding a new dimension to their embrace. Her nails scraping his scalp, her lips sucking his tongue deep into her mouth as she ground into him.

His hands pushed into the delicate lace of her underwear, slipped into her wet sex and he let her set the pace, her hips riding his fingers in a frantic rhythm. He wished they had time to get a condom. He wanted to feel her wet heat surrounding him desperately. But he didn't want to stop. He didn't want to be separated from her for any longer than necessary. Besides, he realized as Maya pushed her arm between their bodies, into his sweatpants and his hips jutted forward, they had time.

They had all the time in the world.

Kenny was rummaging in the refrigerator looking for something to make for lunch. Maya was sitting on the counter next to the sink, eating a bowl of grapes and staring at his ass.

"Didn't I buy some mushrooms before we left?" Kenny called from the fridge.

"Uh huh," she said, even though she literally had no idea. She was daydreaming about pushing his pants down his hips and sucking him into her mouth. She popped another grape into her mouth with a smirk.

There was a knock at her – their – door.

She sighed. "I'll get it."

"Absolutely not," he said, turning around quickly. "Stay here."

She jumped down from the counter and followed him into the living room.

"Didn't I say stay in the kitchen?" He called over his shoulder.

"I'm your backup," she whispered.

"You gonna protect me with a bowl of grapes?"

She frowned. "I'll throw it at their head," she said. He chuckled.

She watched as Kenny checked the peephole and sighed. He turned to her, "You can stand down."

He pulled open the door and ushered whoever was there inside.

Maya recognized him from Hong Kong.

Kenny closed the door and turned to her, "Maya, this is Carlisle. He's in the black ops division."

The man was tall, just a bit taller than Kenny and big. Seeing him in a regular pair of jeans and t-shirt she was struck at how big all of his limbs were. Thick, was the word that immediately came to her mind.

He walked across the carpet and extended his hand to her. "It's nice to meet you. I know Kierra," he said.

She smirked and gripped his hand, "How well?"

Carlisle's entire face and neck turned red.

That was an answer of a sort. "So, are they as wild as we've imagined?"

Kenny exhaled and pulled her hand from Carlisle's. "You've imagined. I don't want to know anything about their sex life." He put an arm around her waist.

"I really can see how you two are friends," Carlisle laughed.

"I assume you're here on business," Kenny said. "Let's get to that."

Carlisle smiled and nodded toward the couch.

They sat, Carlisle at one end, Maya at the other, and Kenny between them.

Before Carlisle could speak, Maya grabbed Kenny's hand and held it in both of hers. "Is it about the hot lady assassin?"

Carlisle nodded. "I chased her into the service hallway, but she was gone in a heartbeat. I found her on hotel security. She was staying on our floor, just down the hall from us."

Kenny's hand tried to clench, but she stroked it until he relaxed.

"We also saw her talking to you," Carlisle aimed at Maya.

"In the spa, outside of the hotel, at the summit cocktail hour and at the closing event."

Maya nodded. "I told you," she said, looking from Carlisle to Kenny. "I just kept running into her. It didn't seem strange at the time."

Kenny nodded reassuringly at her and squeezed her hand.

"You spent that last afternoon together right?" Carlisle asked.

Maya nodded.

"Did she say anything that stuck out to you as odd or significant?"

Maya shook her head immediately. She had been thinking about this ever since Rita had pulled that gun from her purse. The answer was no. "She told me she was a secretary for one of the diplomats. I never even thought to ask who. So stupid," she said.

Kenny cut her off, "No you're not. You had no way of knowing that something was off." He looked at her until she nodded and leaned into his side. He kissed her forehead gently.

When they looked back at Carlisle, his eyes had gone haunted. And it reminded him of the melancholy she'd seen in Rita's eyes.

"She did seem a bit sad sometimes," Maya said hesitantly. "Kind of like she'd lost someone. I don't know, it sounds stupid," she said and then corrected herself. "I don't know if it's important, but the last thing she said to me was that I should be careful because 'Love can make you do crazy things.'"

Carlisle nodded and reached into his jacket pocket. He took out his phone. Kenny and Maya watched as he tapped at it. And then he passed it to Kenny who passed it to her.

"Is this her?" Carlisle asked.

Maya looked at the picture. There were differences certainly. Rita's hair had been straightened and was a bit lighter than the woman in the image whose face was framed by a riot of chocolate curls. Rita had seemed open and warm – sometimes sad – and the woman Maya was looking at had a haughty, but maybe a little playful, look on her face. But those dark brown eyes – warm but piercing – were exactly the same.

"That's her," Maya said. "Definitely."

Carlisle nodded.

"Who is she?" Kenny asked.

Carlisle exhaled. "Technically, she's dead. Although the name on her death certificate, Maria Martinez, is not her real name."

"Do they teach y'all how to be real cryptic or do you just develop that skill on your own?" Maya interjected, aiming the question at Kenny.

Kenny smiled, but kept his eyes on Carlisle.

"Her name's Amrita Salazar. She was one of The Agency's best agents about a decade ago. She disappeared in an op in Mexico about five years ago. We thought she was dead."

"Well clearly she's not," Kenny said, his body tense beside her. No amount of stroking would calm him down. At least not any stroking she could give him while Carlisle was here.

"She worked for The Agency?" Maya whispered. "Then why the hell did she kill that guy?"

Carlisle shook his head. "We don't know yet, but I'm going to find out. In the meantime, I need your help." He aimed the last at Kenny.

"Anything," he replied.

Maya understood the hard flint in Kenny's voice. This wasn't about the mission in Hong Kong. This was about Rita – Amrita, she corrected herself mentally – and how close she'd gotten to Maya.

"I need you to make an introduction," Carlisle said.

Kenny frowned. "To who?"

"To your old partner. Lamont White."

"Why Lamont? Is he in danger?"

Carlisle shook his head. "No, I don't think so. But as it happens, he knows her ex-husband. And there's a really good chance that she might come for him. Now that she's back from the dead."

Other books by
KATRINA JACKSON

<u>Welcome to Sea Port</u>

From Scratch

Inheritance

Small Town Secrets

Her Christmas Cookie

<u>The Spies Who Loved Her</u>

Pink Slip

Private Eye

Bang & Burn

New Year, New We

His Only Valentine

Bright Lights

<u>Erotic Accommodations</u>

Room for Three?

Neighborly

<u>Love At Last</u>

Every New Year

<u>Heist Holidays</u>

Grand Theft N.Y.E.

<u>The Family</u>

Beautiful & Dirty

www.ingramcontent.com/pod-product-compliance
Lightning Source LLC
Chambersburg PA
CBHW071300190726
48292CB00007B/2622